THE RESURRECTION INCIDENT

By

Sheila Lee Brown

ISBN-978-1-946651-12-9

Published by TZ Books
www.tz-books.com

Contents

CHAPTER 1: TIME TO JUMP
JAREM

A panic attack was not a part of the plan. Fists gripped tight, Jarem turned away from the crowd walking the inner circle around the Big Mek space portal. His chest constricted as he struggled to control his breathing.

Breathe in. Breathe out.

Jarem pulled the hood of his cloak further over his face and leaned his shoulder lightly on the outside wall of the shop beside him.

"You okay?" Tock asked from behind.

Jarem gave a quick nod. He didn't want Tock nor the rest of the team to see this or feel this. He was scared. Terrified. They needed him to be more than that. Jarem released his fists and began tightening and releasing different areas of his body. He slowed his breathing as much as he could, remembering that his team surrounded him and that they had been in much more dangerous situations and got out unscathed. He tapped into the feeling of security he felt from them.

I am safe. I. Am. Safe.

After several brief moments that seemed strained and unending, the pressure subsided. Thankfully, the attack had been mild.

"This is where they found you, right?" Nelly whispered next to Jarem. She scanned the surrounding area to make sure no one was listening.

Jarem turned to fully look at his friends, but he wasn't ready to speak yet, so he gave another quick nod. Nelly and Tock stood closest to Jarem. Behind them was the rest of the team. All together, the team was Jarem, Tock, Nelly, Peet, Rema, and Kin—six young Earthers, not long passed puberty and on the brink of adulthood. Old enough to be thinking about a future, and, hopefully, capable enough to create one worth living.

"Over there," Jarem said, softly. He indicated three platforms between two shops further down the inner circle with a quick glance—no reason to point and risk being noticed. On each platform was a different species for sale. And, sure enough, one platform appeared to have half a dozen Earthers sitting on it, waiting to be bought. Jarem knew from experience that a force field surrounded each platform to prevent escape.

"Are you sure you're okay?" Tock asked again.

"I'm fine. A little lightheaded. Just needed to adjust my oxygen aura," Jarem lied.

Tock gave Jarem a long, hard stare, but let it pass. He didn't necessarily believe Jarem, but he also wasn't overly concerned. Jarem was good at covering his emotions from the others. Their feelings were always available to him. Jarem's empathic nature and telepathic ability were his biggest assets to the group. Those abilities had made it possible for them to be together. It also put a lot of pressure on Jarem to live up to some ideal of what the Yacca had seen in him years ago. He wasn't sure he was up for whatever they were going to find at the end of this journey. Just being in Big Mek again was enough to unravel him. It was useful that the other Earthers were all a little nervous, too. It helped to move the focus off Jarem.

"Don't pick at it," Rema whispered to Peet.

Peet's hand stopped just as he was about to rub the blue spot painted on his forehead and instead scratched at his nose. Nelly surveyed their surroundings with her quick, careful eyes and gave the nod that all was clear. No one had noticed.

All six Earthers had the spot painted there, large enough to cover the center part of their forehead. They also had the same blue color running in two lines down both sides of their necks in the manner of Visnaillan beings. Jarem could feel the paint as a tightness across the skin and the temptation to touch it was strong. He didn't dare, as the discovery that it was not a true genetic trait would bring suspicion about who they were, and, more seriously, what they were. One of the luckiest breaks Earthers had was that so many beings looked similar to them and could be easily imitated if you had the right resources. And hiding what they were was absolutely necessary, because being an Earther, most days, was not a lucky thing at all.

A light breeze passed through the avenue and the pungent smells that were wafting through went with it. The neutralizing mist was nice to have in a place where so many species commingled and produced odors that may or may not be appealing to other species.

"Whew! Grateful for that breeze. I was starting to smell myself. Why did you have to spray so much of that pheromone on me? I'm going to have to take five showers to get the stink off!" Peet said.

"Are you trying to ruin this mission by saying things like that?" Rema whispered again and elbowed Peet in the ribs.

"No one can hear me," Peet said with a grin. "Dr. Yac and I added a proximity feature to our comms so that our combined auric field can contain the vibration of sounds."

"Dr. Yac?" Jarem asked.

"That's what I call the Yacca that came with us," Peet said. "I saw the title of Doctor in an Earth book once," he continued speaking, but began making more adjustments to his wrist comms with finger-pressure commands and eye movements. "It describes someone advanced in their field of study."

"We should still be cautious," Nelly said. "Besides, you've smelled worse. Remember Gagua?"

They had found Rema and Peet on the planet Gagua. They had survived by hiding out in the sewer systems and scrounging whatever food they could when they could. For years, they had been each other's only companions after their family was taken.

Rema snorted, and Peet smirked at the jab. That they could find the humor in their past showed how far they had come. Each person on the team had been through horrible things that they never wanted to talk about or remember. But they had. Each one was still going through a process of healing. It was necessary in order to do the work they were doing.

"That may be true," Peet replied. He finished his adjustments and looked at the group. "I'm just worried that some other Visnaillans might pass by when the neutralizer wears off and we'll find ourselves being confronted with a proposal to start a marriage community."

"You're not very attractive by Visnaillan standards," Kin said.

The team turned to look at Kin, surprised at her apparent attempt at a joke. Rema gave Kin a playful nudge and Kin smiled sheepishly. Peet snickered and the rest of the group laughed.

Jarem relaxed as a feeling of camaraderie spread through the Earthers. The team became quiet and settled in to watch the moving crowds and wait. Their energy was less anxious and more hopeful.

The Mekla portal station (aka The Big Mek) was a small city on the planet Hanu. Hanu was the home planet to the Yacca. However, they had deemed their portal technology to be a resource to be shared. They created this domed city as a trading post for travelers. It was a popular jump off point for different species and unlike the rest of the planet, the city operated under the law of the local solar system and not Yacca law. Because of this, the Yacca had limited authority and could not guarantee safety for Earthers despite their desire for that.

The Yacca did not interfere with other species unless challenged and they would also not interfere directly in the fate of Earthers. However, they assisted the Earthers in ways they determined did not violate their code of ethics. Here, a Yacca was gaining portal access for them. The Yaccan representative was less likely to be challenged, and it was important that the Earthers go unnoticed. The Earthers had kept their distance in case things didn't go as planned and they had to get away quickly. That was their default mode of operation and it had served them well.

"It shouldn't be much longer," Jarem reassured them.

Still apprehensive of having another attack, Jarem cleared his mind and focused on his team. He regularly checked in with their energetic and emotional wellbeing. Tock was the heart of the group and kept them all together. He had been with Jarem at the beginning of this project, the mission to preserve and save Earthenkind. Nelly, standing next to Tock, had also been there since the beginning. She and Tock had become more and more inseparable over the last two years. If they weren't on a mission, they were always together. Nelly wanted to save everyone and she was a force to be reckoned with in any situation. She was a true warrior and watched everyone's back. Next to Nelly were Rema and Peet, a sister and brother. They had joined the team seven missions ago. Siblings were a rarity amongst Earthers, as few families ever survived to produce more than one child. The last member of the group was Kin—she was quiet, capable, and nearly as good an intuitive empath and psychic as Jarem.

Passage has been procured. Begin making your way to the portal.

The voice in Jarem's head was the Yacca representative that had volunteered to help his team get portal access. Dr. Yac, as Peet called him. Jarem was the only Earther able to communicate with the Yacca telepathically. Having Yaccas willing to help the Earthers was another lucky break. If everything worked out as Jarem hoped, Earthers wouldn't have to rely on luck so often. If they could find what they were looking for, maybe they could even return home - to Earth itself.

"It's done," Jarem told the group. "Time to jump."

The Earthers shifted into mission mode and began walking down the avenue with others heading towards the portal. They walked in two columns of three, mimicking the orderly style of Visnaillans, not moving too fast and attempting to blend in. Jarem and Tock were at the head of each column. Jarem could sense the uneasiness building again in the group as they neared the platform with the Earthers for sale. He sent out a telepathic wave of assurance that he felt about their progress and what they would accomplish on this mission. Jarem felt the uneasiness wane as assurance was reciprocated back to him. He needed it as well. He felt like his outward calm was teetering on the edge of collapse.

"We're being watched." Nelly's whisper came from behind Jarem. "The market by the Earthers."

Jarem stopped at a shop just past the platforms and glanced around as if noticing the wares. He picked up on the ill intent of the being before even seeing its cold, unreadable eyes staring at them from behind the platform.

"Got him," Jarem said. He even recognized it - an insect-like humanoid called Sloctum. Jarem eyed the distance to the portal's entryway. Even at a full run, it would take them at least ten long breaths to get there. And that wasn't the type of attention they would want

SHEILA LEE BROWN

to draw to themselves, anyway. Jarem waved away a
vendor with four arms, attempting to show off some
stone bracelets that it claimed were the tech of
ancient creators. Jarem led the group to the head of a
cul-de-sac between two shops, where they would be
far enough away from others to talk safely.

"Look how many Earthers there are," Nelly said, trying
not to glance over at their frightened faces. "We
should do something to help them."

"We can't save them and portal jump," Rema replied.
"We knew there would be risk of this when we came
here. Soon we'll be able to help all of them, but we're
not prepared for a rescue mission."

Nelly frowned. Jarem didn't like it either. Over the past
three years, they had spent a lot of time rescuing and
helping fellow Earthers, though they had been
becoming more and more scarce these days. Hidden
deep within Hanu, they had upwards of two thousand
Earth humans creating a small society and attempting
to heal some of the trauma they had lived through for
nearly eight generations. As long as they were under
the protection of the Yacca, they were safe from
ending up on the selling block. But that didn't mean
they were completely safe. The biggest danger to
Earthers was not the various beings that were taking
advantage of them in their unfortunate situation. That
was simply a side problem.

"We don't even know if they are true Earthers," Peet added.

"He's right," Tock agreed.

Nelly grunted, but didn't press the issue.

"We need to focus on the being watching us for the moment," Jarem said. "I recognize him. He specializes in selling Earthers - sometimes as pets and sometimes for slaughter-trials." Jarem felt several jolts of anger from the group. "If he is watching us, he might suspect...," Jarem didn't dare finish the sentence, "I'm going to hang back and see if I can find out what he wants. You all should keep walking to the portal."

"I don't think that is a good idea," Nelly started. "We should all get to the portal as quickly as possible and get out of here. Or let me find out what he wants."

"And what if he follows us through?" Jarem asked. "We can't risk everything. I have the most experience reading other beings. It has to be me that talks to him." Jarem felt a pit in his stomach at the words. He wished someone else could do it. He clenched his fists inside his cloak to keep his hands from shaking.

The rest of the team nodded, however, they weren't happy about it. Jarem sent them an energetic wave of his determination. He felt it was weaker than it should have been. It must have been enough because the team began walking in two columns again down the middle of the avenue as Jarem hung back and began examining some Earthwares around an antique shop. The vendor had a hologram of the planet Earth just above the merchandise. Apparently it was trendy to scavenge a planet and profit from the misfortune of its native beings. Jarem looked over the objects, which ranged from metal eating utensils to preserved wooden furniture. This vendor even had fruits and vegetables that it claimed were from Earth. Jarem didn't recognize any of them. But he had never been to Earth before. No human that he had ever known had been. An Earth human trying to go home had a death wish. A worse-than-death wish.

Life had seemed to be mostly about death to Jarem until he met the Yacca. He remembered standing on the selling block, feeling small and cold, grieving the loss of his mother, almost not caring if they sold him for slaughter trials. He happened to look up as a group of three Yaccas passed, and that moment had changed his life.

Jarem had been the first Earther the Yacca took in. Afterwards, they had gotten curious about his species and had sent missions to the planet. They would bring back various things that they felt would be useful, but the planet no longer had Earth-evolved humans on it. Based on the images the Yacca had showed them, Earth was a beautiful planet. Jarem hoped that the work they were doing now would allow them, or maybe the next generation, to get back there.

"Interested in Earther artifacts?"

Jarem recognized the high-pitched voice even as his comms adjusted to translate. He didn't even have to look to see that Sloctum had made his way over to him.

"Merely curiosity," Jarem replied.

"Of course." The voice moved closer and Jarem felt the point of something on his side. "Careful now," Sloctum said. "We don't want any damages, do we? Come."

Jarem put down the piece of Earth metal he was examining and allowed himself to be led through the crowd to another cul-de-sac between shops. He could feel his heart racing, wondering what he was thinking to put himself in this situation. And then he felt something else from Sloctum that surprised him. He felt familiarity. Jarem drew a deep breath before speaking.

"What's this about? The station security does not respond well to thieves." Thankfully, he sounded steadier than he felt.

Sloctum released Jarem. Jarem turned to face him. Sloctum stood about the same height as Jarem. Jarem had always found it difficult to look at an insectoid's face. It was hard to read emotion there. And it was a particular challenge to stare into Sloctum's face - the face that had captured him after his mother's death and sold him to the Yacca in this very portal. Other than the insect-face, shelled back and exoskeleton, Sloctum had two arms and two legs like most evolved beings.

"I remember all the Earthers that I sell," Sloctum said. "I catalogue their appearance, smell, and…," a proboscis whipped out from between Sloctum's mandibles and grazed Jarem's cheek, "even taste."

Jarem pulled away, but Sloctum had a tight hold on him.

"I sold you nearly six growth seasons ago. Got away, did you?" Sloctum poked the blue spot on Jarem's forehead with a clawed hand. "I'm guessing if you're pretending to be a Visnaillan, chances are that your friends are Earthers, too. Visnals rarely consort outside their kind."

Jarem's body tensed. This was worse than he thought. He took another deep breath. Fear ran its sharp claws down his spine. But he had also been preparing for a situation like this.

"What do you want?" he asked.

"Not going to deny it? Good. We don't have time for that."

"What does that mean?"

"It's lucky for you that I came along, Earther. I'm doing you a favor." Sloctum ran a claw across one of his antennae. "Get your friends and come with me. I have a buyer that will pay top money for Earthers in such good condition."

"Some favor. Why would I go with you?"

"A cluster of resurrects has been spotted heading this way." Sloctum's mandible twitched. "You know what that means?"

Jarem felt a chill creep up his spine. If that was true, he needed to reach his team and get out of there as quickly as possible. He also thought of the other Earthers that were being sold in the avenue. They wouldn't stand a chance against the resurrects.

"You're lying," Jarem said, but even as he said it, he could feel that Sloctum was telling the truth. Jarem felt the pressure building in his chest again.

"We don't have much time," Sloctum said. "This will be easier if you don't resist."

"What d-"

Jarem felt something in his mind, a tendril of something that didn't originate from him. Sloctum was going to control him, try to make him betray his friends and then sell them. It gave Jarem a focus to shift away from his fear. Sloctum was in for a surprise.

Your team is here. Do you need assistance?

Jarem grimaced. Dr. Yac would try to communicate with him when he needed to concentrate.

I'm on my way, Jarem sent back to Dr. Yac. He then took another deep breath, pushed his fear aside as best he could, and felt himself get close enough to his center to act. The tendril of something foreign was still there in his mind. He supposed that for most traumatized Earthers, Sloctum's feeble attempt to infiltrate their psyche might work. Jarem and his team were not the typical Earthers that Sloctum encountered. He took one more slow breath before stepping forward into action.

Sloctum barely had a moment to twitch before Jarem flicked the tendril away from his mind and then pushed it back to Sloctum with his own telepathic surge. At the same time the wave of Jarem's mental punch crashed into Sloctum, Jarem moved forward and down, spinning to kick the back joint of the insectoid's leg. Sloctum collapsed, his expression a mixture of astonishment and grogginess. Jarem rolled behind Sloctum and stood over the downed creature, placing his hand on its hard skull casing. *You did not see us, we did not speak,* Jarem pressed into its mind. He felt Sloctum trying to fight it, but the element of surprise had worked in Jarem's favor. Sloctum fell over in a daze as Jarem hurried back onto the avenue and towards the portal. He forced himself to not walk too fast.

The portal access points were a series of arches at the end of the avenue that were programmed to take beings to different areas of the universe without having to use spacecraft. Jarem saw Dr. Yac and his team near an arch, waiting for Jarem with one of the portal programmers, another Yacca. Dr. Yac was slightly taller than the Earthers with an enlarged head and eyes and bluish-purple skin. A force field surrounded the portals so that only paying customers could get in to use them.

Resurrects are coming, Jarem sent to Dr. Yac. Dr. Yac's skin darkened slightly and he turned to speak to the team. Jarem didn't need to be near them to sense their alarm. It took all his effort not to scream. Jarem increased his speed. Nelly was gesturing wildly and Tock was talking to her calmly, attempting to maintain control of the situation as Jarem made his way to the portal gate. Dr. Yac indicated he was a part of his group and Jarem entered and walked over to his team. The portal programmer began completing adjustments to the portal they were going to use.

"Is it true? They're coming?" Nelly whispered as Jarem approached. Jarem nodded. "We can't leave those Earthers here. We have to do something."

"I have no idea how much time we have," Jarem said. "They could be here any moment."

As if on cue, an alarm went off in the portal station. Resurrects had no sense of proper entry ways and often triggered defense systems when they showed up and forced their way through. Nothing seemed to stop them, as if they somehow defied technology.

"It's happening," Nelly said. "If they have made it through the entrance, they'll be here soon."

"I'll help the Earthers," Tock said. "You all go through the portal."

"I'll go with you," Nelly said and moved to go.

"No," Tock said, holding her back. Nelly glared at him, but Tock looked her in the eye. "Jarem has to finish the mission. He needs *you* to have his back."

"I'll help Tock," Rema offered. "Traumatized Earthers respond well to me. But it would be better if we had some more mental juice." Rema looked over at Kin. Kin nodded.

Jarem looked over his team. Rema and Kin had moved over to join Tock. Nelly had reluctantly stepped over to join Jarem and Peet.

"We're split in half," Jarem said. "Is this what everyone wants?"

"It's not ideal. And it's not the plan, but Nelly's right. If we don't try to help the others, who are we?" Tock said. "Why are we even doing what we're doing?"

They looked at each other in silence.

"Let's make it count," Jarem finally said. "We know what is possible from what we are doing today."

Tock nodded. He and Nelly shared one last long look before he led Rema and Kin out the portal gate and towards the Earther selling block. Several were yelling for help. Kin looked as afraid as Jarem felt. Rema grabbed her hand, and the three darted down the avenue towards the platform. That's when Jarem saw them, the resurrects, floating nearly a head span above the walking surface at the far end of the avenue. He felt his throat constrict and his body trembled.

These creatures were Earthers before they were destroyed and reborn into this twisted form. Jarem had seen it happen up close once. He had hidden in a wall, but he could see through a crack in the panel. It looked like some force had entered a body that could not contain it, and the limbs exploded from the torso as it adjusted its fit. Then, the same force pulled the limbs back into place. The person inside was no longer there. The eyes filled with blood and took on a crimson glow. Jarem felt Nelly grip his arm, and he bent over and vomited before he could stop himself.

"We've got to move," Nelly said. Jarem was still gagging as she pulled him away towards Dr. Yac and Peet. "Do you really think they can get them and escape?" Her fear was evident.

"It's Tock," Peet said. "And no resurrect is as stubborn as Rema." He couldn't keep a tremor out of his voice.

"It will all be for nothing if we don't go now," Jarem whispered. He wasn't sure how he had vomited when his throat felt so tight. Nelly was still propping him up. Jarem didn't like that he was leaving half his crew, but their window of opportunity was small. He stood up and turned towards the portal. He had thought he would be more ready when he saw them again, but he would have been lying if he said he wasn't glad for a quick escape. "I can stand now."

Nelly released her hold on Jarem. They turned towards their designated portal arch, which seemed quite large up close. Each arch stood nearly three times Jarem's height, and it was wide enough for at least six Earthers to go through side by side. But now there was only going to be three.

"Everything set?" she asked Dr. Yac.

Dr. Yac nodded in the affirmative.

"Let's go."

That was Jarem. Nelly looked back to the avenue, trying to locate Tock, but many of the beings were moving out of the way of the resurrects as they floated their way towards the selling block. Some were eagerly pointing to the selling block and trying to make their way over to watch the spectacle about to happen. Almost absentmindedly, Nelly said, "The right thing is not always the easy thing." It was something Jarem had heard Tock say several times when helping others. Without waiting for a response, Nelly abruptly turned and walked through the portal.

Peet followed more slowly. Jarem and Dr. Yac shared a concerned glance.

"Are we doing the right thing?" Jarem asked. He wanted more than anything to walk through the portal and to safety, but it didn't feel good to leave three of his friends in danger.

"You are in control of your future," Dr. Yac replied. "I am only here to assist with the portal and to make observations."

Jarem nodded and slowly turned away from the chaos erupting in the marketplace. He and Dr. Yac stepped through the portal just as the screams escalated.

CHAPTER 2: INTO THE DARK
ZELWA

Zelwa coughed as a breeze shifted the dust coating everything on Laris into a light orange cloud that tickled her face and dried out her throat.

"Pull up your neck gaiter."

The voice was muffled. Zelwa turned to see her mother walking up behind her, neck gaiter pulled up snug over her nose and mouth. Zelwa cleared her throat. Her mom had barely said anything to her since they had arrived on Laris, except to tell her what to do. Zelwa had grown slightly taller than her mom over the past year and wasn't a fan of taking orders like she was still a child.

"Didn't you test the dust? It's harmless, other than being a bit irritating." Zelwa brushed some dust off the sleeves of her uniform. "Besides, we're almost to the ship."

"Suit yourself, Zelwa," her mother said, and walked by her at a quicker pace, leaving Zelwa behind as she turned a curve in the path that wound through several large rock formations.

Zelwa coughed again as another dust cloud swirled around her. She yanked up her neck gaiter over her mouth and began walking faster. The path was just big enough for two supply carts to pass one another. None were in sight at the moment. As Zelwa rounded the curve, she could see the ship maybe a hundred yards down the hill, a large metallic disc amongst the planet's rocky surface, big enough to accommodate the two hundred and eight people that had made the choice to join Zelwa's parents on the voyage to study Laris. A quick walk down the hill and Zelwa would be at its opening. She hesitated. She could see her mother already halfway down and heading towards the loading ramp, which was currently an unloading ramp as supplies and useful equipment were being removed from the ship. Zelwa's father would be somewhere inside, organizing the unloading.

Zelwa reminded herself that she had made the choice to come on this expedition. She could have stayed with her dad's sister and her family and had a somewhat normal life. Maybe that would have been easier. That's not what had happened. Zelwa had thought that staying with her parents would help them. And help her. Before the decision to come to Laris, things hadn't been great in her family. Zelwa's counselor had once said something about all wounds healing with time. How would she know unless she was with her parents when it happened? So, Zelwa hopped onboard the research ship with her mom and dad and they made their way to the planet Laris.

"Are we done yet?" Mora groaned as she popped up beside Zelwa and lay her head on Zelwa's shoulder, her long hair spilling down Zelwa's back. Mora had her face covering up. But then, she was usually more responsible than Zelwa. And smarter. Mora and Zelwa were the only teenagers on this expedition, however, some of the crew members had toddlers.

"It will probably take us all week to get the ship cleared," Zelwa said. "Are we even still measuring time in Earth weeks?"

"The days here are pretty close in length to Earth's, so why not?" Mora said. She lifted her head off Zelwa and grinned. "You want to race down?"

"Not real--,"

Mora took off running down the hill. Zelwa followed after a brief hesitation because—what else did she have to do? Besides helping move all usable equipment and personal items off the ship and into the planet's caves, that is. Zelwa skidded to a stop several feet from the ship.

"Save some of that energy for the work at hand," a gruff voice said from behind Zelwa. She turned to see Jonah, one of her dad's assistants. He had a strong reputation for getting things done. At the moment, there was a lot that needed to get done and he had the look of someone about to delegate tasks.

"I have to go clear my room," Zelwa said quickly and darted away before Jonah could assign her anything more strenuous. She passed her mom, talking to another crew member about food and water sources, and caught up with Mora in the passageway leading to each of their family's living quarters.

"We're still leaving so much behind," Zelwa said.

"Doesn't work, anyway. Or won't for long," Mora replied. "If we ever get a response from Earth..."

"Someone will come looking for us."

"Maybe." Mora smiled at Zelwa. "We'll be okay. Besides, what we're learning from Elder will benefit everyone back home. Who knows, we may even figure out a new way to get this hunk of junk juiced up again."

The light above them flickered, but stayed on. They had encountered some major damage that Zelwa didn't quite understand. Elder had no interest in anything electrical and did not offer any help on the repair, however, he showed concern about their wellbeing and offered an alternative—the caves. Elder had created them himself. He had an unusual affinity with the planet and could shift its resources to his needs. Of course, the only resources on Laris seemed to be rocks and dust.

"We may not have a week's worth of power left," Zelwa said as she neared the entry to her parent's compartment.

"Then we better get everything to the caves."

Zelwa jumped as her mom appeared behind the two girls.

"Hi, Dr. Wissinger," Mora said. "Excuse me. I have to go find my mom." Mora walked off in a hurry.

"Wait, Mora," Dr. Wissinger said. "I wanted to check in on you both. I understand you're taking extra lessons with Elder."

"That's right," Mora replied. She exchanged a concerned look with Zelwa. Zelwa shrugged.

"You're not in trouble. I just wanted to find out how things are going. Elder tells me you two are having success where the rest of us are struggling."

"Elder says our minds are more flexible because we are...uh..."

"Younger? It's not unexpected that our younger folk would catch on more quickly. Perhaps we should have encouraged more families with teenagers to come. The smaller children aren't quite ready for the training."

"Yes, well—" Mora began.

"Have both of you completed an Impressing?"

"We have."

"Good. Mora, find your mother. Zelwa, let's see what's left to be moved out."

Zelwa had watched her mom warily during the exchange. Dr. Annette Wissinger could be intimidating, and it was a peculiar thing for Zelwa to see her mom interacting with others on a mission. Her mother was so matter of fact, so accustomed to being in charge and having people do whatever she told them. It differed from how Zelwa had seen her before the mission, when most of the time she stayed in her room, curled up in her bed like a wilting flower.

Mora scurried away, and Zelwa turned and entered the compartment without speaking to her mother. She didn't know what to say to her, anyway. Zelwa walked through the small living area and kitchenette with a food matrix that was powered down to conserve energy. Towards the back were three doorways. Her parents' room was on the right. The room on the left was Zelwa's. In the middle was the shower and toilet. Zelwa ducked into her room. She heard her mother follow her into the living area, but she said nothing to Zelwa. Things still felt weird between them. Zelwa had hoped that coming to Laris with her parents would give them an opportunity to heal and maybe grow closer. Zelwa had made a few efforts, but nothing had changed. Now Zelwa was beginning to not care.

Inside her room, Zelwa plopped down on the full-sized bed and kicked at one of several gray containers filled with her personal items. The room was already nearly as empty as when she had moved in. Everything from her desk was in a container. She had pulled most of her uniforms out of the closet. They were already feeling snug with the height she had gained. Zelwa lay back on the mattress and sighed. The process of moving into the caves felt rushed. After all, the ship would still be here on the planet's surface. They could always come back to it to get anything they needed. Elder had been insistent. He was wary of outsiders, but for whatever reason, he *allowed* them to be there. As the only being on Laris, Elder himself was a bit of a mystery. The planet had no insects or other small creatures, or even plant life on the surface. Both Dr. Wissingers, Zelwa's mom and dad, loved the mystery he and his teachings presented.

"The last cart will head to the caves within the hour, so make sure you have what you want for the day with you."

Startled, Zelwa sat up at the sound of her mother's voice. She was standing in Zelwa's doorway. Her statement was no-nonsense and did not seem to be an opening to talk. Sometimes Zelwa felt her mom forgot she was her daughter and not just another member of the crew.

"I'm almost done," Zelwa said. Not expecting any further conversation, Zelwa moved to open the cabinets and drawers one by one to make sure they were empty.

"What's it like?"

Zelwa turned, surprised that her mom was still standing in her doorway.

"What?"

"The Impressing."

"I don't know how to describe it," Zelwa said slowly. Her mom's voice sounded less authoritative and softer. Zelwa noticed she was holding something in her hand. It glinted in the light—a small picture in a metallic frame. Zelwa froze, recognizing the reason for the change in mood. She chose her words carefully, not sure how to navigate around a conversation she'd been waiting to have for a long time, but now wasn't sure she was ready for.

"When you feel the connection…there's an opportunity to create with it," Zelwa said.

"What did you Impress?"

"It was nothing, really." Zelwa turned back to her things and moved a couple of shirts around in her tub. "We were just practicing."

"A memory."

Zelwa couldn't tell if that was a question or statement. She glanced at her mom. She was looking down at the floor, not at Zelwa. Zelwa focused on the picture frame because it was too hard to look at her mom's face. She could just make out part of the picture from the angle it was being held—the bright yellow of a small uniform.

"Yes, a memory," Zelwa said slowly. But not the one she was sure her mom was thinking about. Never that one.

"How did it feel? Did it change how you saw the memory? Did it make you feel the memory less?"

"Not really," Zelwa spoke even more carefully. They were getting dangerously close to the source of their disconnect. It was a strange feeling. Zelwa thought about how often she had wanted to talk about it, but now it was being forced on her when she wasn't ready, and that was annoying. It felt like the eyes in the photo were now watching her.

"I see," her mother said. "I was wondering..."

Zelwa felt her body tense. What had gotten into her mom? She had barely spoken to her since they had arrived on Laris and now...and now it felt like she wanted to rip open the wound before it was ready to be exposed.

"No," Zelwa said quickly. Too quickly. Her mom looked up. "We're not doing this."

"Zelwa..."

Zelwa turned, snapped the last two containers closed, then lifted them, one on top of the other, to carry out. They were slightly heavier than they looked, but manageable. She was shaking on the inside and wanted to get out before her mom said anything else.

"I have to make sure my things are on the last cart." Her words were curt, and, she hoped, left no opening for further exchange.

"Zelwa..."

"Let. Me. Go."

Zelwa stood firm and her mom took a step back and let her pass, pulling the framed picture up to her chest, the image facing her body so Zelwa couldn't see it. Zelwa was glad. She could see the hurt in her mom's eyes, but she kept moving. All this time she had wanted her mom and dad to talk to her and they hadn't. It wasn't fair or right. Zelwa wasn't ready now. And she didn't want to be forced into it, either.

Zelwa walked out into the passageway and towards the loading ramp, passing others walking into the ship to their own domiciles. Zelwa placed her bins on the cart and darted away before Jonah noticed her again. She walked back up the hill and into the curve with the large rocks. Finding a familiar foothold, she pulled herself up. She continued to climb up and through the openings until she found a nook in the rock where she could pull herself in. Zelwa had stumbled upon this little cubby not long after she and Mora began exploring the planet. No one could see her from below.

Zelwa huddled up even though there was room to stretch out. What was her mom thinking? Zelwa tried not to envision the face she had glimpsed in the framed photo before it was turned from her. It hurt too much. She felt tears streaming down her cheeks and onto her crossed arms. She didn't want to think about it, but it was too late. The face was there in her mind, just as it was often in her dreams and nightmares. Zelwa hugged herself tightly, the way she wished her parents had hugged her the last time she had had seen that face - the face of Timon, her brother. Her dead brother.

CHAPTER 3: SOMETHING IS COMING
JAREM

Stepping through the portal was like stepping through a doorway into another room. The arch on the other side was the same as the one from Big Mek. Once the Yacca had traveled to a location through the portal, they set up a portal station so anyone staying had control to portal back or even to portal to another location.

The connection between the two portals ended as Dr. Yac and Jarem took several steps into their destination, the Gogli portal station. This side of the portal only had one access point and not the triangle. Nelly and Peet were standing nearby with the portal attendant that looked like a large reddish-brown ant.

Gogli differed from the Big Mek. Instead of shops and avenues, it was a simple room with a high ceiling and large doors on one side that presumably led to a hangar with spacecraft. Several other antlike insectoid beings, half the height of the Earthers, scurried about in and out moving cargo that had passed through the portal earlier.

"Please exit," the portal attendant said. His voice had a soothing buzz to it. It stood almost as tall as Nelly, which was slightly larger than the other ant-creatures moving about. It gestured to the doors with its claw. "Have a pleasant experience."

The contrast of this portal to what they just left was jolting. It felt surreal. Jarem and his team had never used the portal system before, always only going as far as a spacecraft and their knowledge of the area would allow. Jarem looked at Nelly and Peet. Nelly looked back at the portal. Peet was looking down at his comms and blinking. Jarem wasn't sure if he was checking on things or avoiding thinking about what had just happened. They both felt anxious. Jarem could feel his own fear in the pit of his stomach. But *they* were safe. The mission was still on track. Who knew what was happening to the others right now?

"We require a ship rental," Dr. Yac said to the portal attendant.

"This can be managed outside the container," the portal attendant said, gesturing to the doors again. "Someone will help you there."

Dr. Yac nodded.

"Shall we continue?" Dr. Yac asked Jarem. Jarem slowly nodded in the affirmative. Nelly put her hand on Jarem's shoulder.

"Maybe we should go back," she said. Peet looked up from his comms.

"Nelly...," Jarem began.

"What if we can't succeed without everyone on the team?" Nelly asked. Jarem had already had that thought as well.

"We have to consider that our information is time sensitive," Peet said. "If we go back, and somehow survive, we don't know if we'll have another opportunity." He looked back down at his comms and sighed. "There are no good choices."

Jarem could feel Nelly's pain and helplessness. It made him question again if they were doing the right thing. Her hand slipped off Jarem's shoulder and he turned to her.

Before he could speak, the sound of the portal opening once more startled them. Even the portal attendant raised his arms in surprise. Jarem tensed as someone stepped through. It was Rema. She had one of the Earthers from the selling block with her. Jarem, Nelly, and Peet rushed over. Peet grabbed his sister's shoulder, then hugged her fiercely. Rema was shaking, her eyes wide.

"Close the portal, NOW!" she screamed at the antlike being.

"NO!" Nelly yelled. "What about Tock? And Kin?"

Rema quickly stepped away from the portal, pushing the unknown Earther ahead of her. The Earther seemed stunned and wary.

"CLOSE IT!"

Nelly rushed over to the open portal, looking through to locate Tock. Jarem followed, worried that she might try to go through. Tock was nowhere in sight. But that's when Jarem saw it, the only plausible reason for Rema's terror.

Floating casually towards the portal was Kin, except it wasn't Kin. The red of the eyes gave it away. The resurrects had gotten her, but something wasn't right. Something was different.

"What happened?" Jarem asked, his eyes still locked on what he now thought of as the Kin-resurrect.

"CLOSE IT! CLOSE IT NOW!"

Peet was holding Rema, but she was struggling to reach the portal attendant to get him to close the portal.

"She's not torn," Nelly said. "Her body isn't torn."

The thing that was not Kin stretched its arms and fingers and neck as if adjusting its fit. Jarem had never seen or heard of resurrects moving like that. They usually just floated around, their limbs bobbing slightly with their movement, the separation of their body parts held together by something unseen. Yet, they moved against defenses as if they could slow time. However, that only happened in spurts. When typically moving, they appeared to move at the normal speed of most beings. And they never needed to touch

40

anything. They merely hovered near an Earther and then took control, almost as if transmitting an energetic wave of destruction and rebirth.

This one looked like it had control of fine motor function. It looked over at the portal and Jarem froze. There was something there in the red glow of the eyes that scared Jarem more than anything else—it was awareness. No one could communicate with resurrects. They didn't even make sense in the grand scheme of things. But this was different. The thing that wasn't Kin smiled and began floating towards the portal, then slowly descended and took a few tentative steps on the ground.

"Close it," Jarem said.

The thing that wasn't Kin tilted its head, watching Jarem through the portal as it approached. The smile grew to a hungry grin. The thing that wasn't Kin reached out—still far from the portal - and Jarem felt a slight pushing at something within. It differed from anything he had experienced with other beings. This wasn't an attack on his mind, it was a full-out attack on his energetic body. He felt the push growing stronger and knew he was going to have to do something and do it fast. As he frantically contemplated his options while energetically hanging on to his body, the portal blinked out.

Jarem gasped for air.

"What was that?"

"They got Kin," Rema said, through her tears. "They got her."

"What about Tock?" Nelly asked urgently. "Did he get away?"

"I don't know," Rema said. She leaned onto Peet, who was standing close to her, and began sobbing. Peet held her as he looked to Jarem for what to do next.

"We have to help Tock," Nelly said.

"Did you just see that?" Jarem asked. "I don't know how to fight it. We need to make sure it can't reopen the portal and come through." Jarem turned to the portal attendant. He could feel Nelly's anger, but if they didn't make the right choices, this could be the end of everything. "Can we do that?"

"No more distress," the portal attendant said. "Please experience calmness."

"Can you stop the portal opening from that location?" Dr. Yac asked. "I will compensate you for any losses."

"We do not receive from that portal often," the portal attendant said. "We mostly import cargo for trade as it is desolate in this area."

"In that case, please ensure that no one can open it from there. What is your fee?"

The portal attendant bowed his head.

"No need," it said. "The goodwill of a Yaccan is its own reward."

Dr. Yac bowed his head in acknowledgement. The portal attendant walked over to the portal and began making adjustments.

Jarem looked around at what remained of his team. Rema had stopped crying, but he could see and feel that she was far from okay. Nelly was about to boil over from anger and frustration. Peet appeared okay, but Jarem could see he was gripping Rema as if she was an anchor to his calm. Dr. Yak remained neutral, as usual. The newly found Earther just stood there, eyeing everyone. They had lost Kin. Tock may be lost as well. In one fell swoop, the entire foundation of their team was nearly destroyed. Only one direction remained.

"This isn't an easy thing to say," Jarem finally said, "but we have to go."

A long silence followed. Jarem could feel the collective grieving, but they also didn't have the luxury of much time.

After a few more moments, Rema slowly nodded as if coming out of a fog and began pushing the Earther she'd saved ahead of her. The poor man seemed confused. He was older than Jarem and his team and wore a mix of materials in layers of white and brown. Peet followed Rema. Nelly stood watching the portal as if expecting it to open again and Tock would pop out.

"I understand the caution. I do," Nelly said in a low voice. "But what if the portal is Tock's only escape?"

"If Tock is still alive, it would be best for him to hide out and then make his way back to the Underground."

"He wouldn't do that," Nelly said. "He would want to find us. And he wouldn't want to risk leading the resurrects to the others."

"Nelly, I am worried about Tock, too," Jarem said. "That thing is waiting out by the portal. We can't get through. The only option we have is to keep pushing

44

forward. You know the window of opportunity is always small."

For a moment, Jarem thought Nelly might decide to stay put at Gogli and further break the team. He watched her face contorting as it went through varying emotions of pain and anger and finally ended in determination. Nelly looked to Jarem and gave a quick nod. They walked out together.

Jarem tried to process the experience as they waited for Dr. Yac to arrange spacecraft travel. He noticed the ant beings moving cargo and organizing it. This planet looked like it served as some sort of warehouse, and the ants passed things through the portal to different destinations. Several small spacecraft lined one side of the facility. They had such a simple purpose. Jarem couldn't help but feel like the closer they got to their goal, the more challenges they might face. Why did he ever think it would be simple? Experience had taught him otherwise.

"We can depart now," Dr. Yac told the group. "It will take us several hours to reach the destination. You all need rest."

Dr. Yac's skin deepened in color. Jarem could feel its concern. They were all depleted of energy. Rema was talking to the new Earther. Jarem was curious about him but didn't feel up to having a conversation at the moment. Rest sounded good. Dr. Yac motioned to a small ship nearby.

"Let's go, then," Jarem said.

CHAPTER 4: THE IMPRESSING
ZELWA

Zelwa found the caves of Laris quite interesting. Elder had created a magnificent labyrinth of caves. Elder himself looked like a large version of an Earth human, maybe twice the size of Zelwa's dad. His facial features were soft and feminine, but his body seemed masculine. He explained the nature of his existence was complex and they could refer to him as a man for simplicity. Zelwa liked him. He was patient and kind. Elder told them he liked his privacy, but he also liked the process of creating. He had taken an interest in Zelwa and Mora and gave them extra lessons on working with the planet's stone.

"As you attune to the environment of Laris, you will feel the vibration of the stones more and more. If you can match that vibration, you've created a current. Within that current, you can Impress information into the stone or receive it, although the planet may not have much to share that would be of interest to beings that exist in form so briefly."

"Thanks for reminding us," Mora snorted. She was picking up and looking over several stones on a stone table in the center of the room. "We're still young, and will be around for a while, I hope."

Zelwa was silent. She knew that being young had nothing to do with how long a person might be around. Instead, she looked down at the stone in her hand, wondering what knowledge she could impart. The stone was slightly oval and oblong with a blue-gray shine. The stones in this room were smooth, unlike the stones of the surface with their rough edges. More of Elder's work.

Zelwa and Mora were with Elder in a circular cavern chamber that was lined with shelves. Zelwa was present when Elder caused the shelves to grow to the dimensions he required. This room was where they practiced Impressing. Impressing was the process of embedding memories or other information into the minerals of the stone. Elder had named this room the Chamber of Remembrance and successful crew members had filled the stones on the shelves with memories. Most of the stones belonged to Mora and Zelwa.

"Why should we Impress our memories?" Zelwa asked.

"This is just to build your ability for future manipulation," Elder said. "Impressing your memories and retrieving them is one of the simplest ways to develop an affinity with the minerals. It should also provide some energetic separation for anything traumatic if you wish to Impress it."

Zelwa could feel Elder's gaze. That was the thing about these advanced beings. They knew things. At least Elder was respectful enough to not probe her mind. At least, she thought he hadn't. Would she even know?

"Will we be able to make rooms like this?" Mora asked.

"Perhaps," Elder said. "I don't fully know the extent of what you will find possible. That makes this experiment interesting."

"Is that why you let us come here?" Mora asked, looking up at Elder. "We're an interesting experiment? Were you bored here by yourself?"

Zelwa felt like Mora was talking too much. Why did people need to ask so many questions? Did the answers even change anything?

"I do not experience what you describe as boredom," Elder said. "But you appear to be experiencing that now. Should we try again another time?"

"No," Mora said. "I've picked a stone and I'm ready." She held up a light gray rock with flecks of something shiny reflecting the light coming from the glowing rock in the ceiling. "How about you, Zelwa?"

Zelwa thought about her interaction with her mother the day before. What if Impressing was a real option to feel less hurt? Less angry? A stone seemed like a safe thing to confide in. She still was nervous. She would have to relive the memory if she Impressed it. And would some of the other crew try to see it? Would her mother? That idea made her uncomfortable. She was curious. Would the Impressing alleviate any of the surrounding distress? Her mother and father hadn't helped. Maybe this was the therapy she needed.

Maybe if she Impressed it into the stone, it wouldn't plague her mind. Maybe she could even be a better daughter.

Zelwa nodded an affirmative.

"Then let's begin. Focus," Elder said.

Zelwa placed the stone on the table in front of her, cupping her hands around it as she gazed down at its smooth blue-gray surface. Touching the stone wasn't necessary for impressing, but Zelwa found it helpful. The last few Impressings had been simple memories—a birthday party when she was seven, playing with a puppy at the park, finding her favorite purple octopus plushie under her bed when she thought her parents had taken it.

Zelwa looked at the stone as if it was the only thing that existed. And then it felt like the memory was already pushing its way forward, wanting to be freed. Zelwa forced it to the side and focused on getting in tune with the stone. It wasn't a quick process. She wondered how Mora was doing but nudged that distracting thought to the side as well. It was fascinating to Zelwa how, after several long moments of focusing on the stone, she could almost feel the hardness of its makeup—and not just with touch. She could feel it in her mind. And, after several long moments of paying attention to that, she could feel the spaces in between the hardness. Then, even longer moments later, she could feel what was connecting all the pieces of the stone and holding it into its current form. She almost had a sense of how Elder could manipulate it, but she was close to her purpose and didn't want to bungle it.

And there it was. Something hard to explain, but it felt like Zelwa's mind tapped into some part of the internal workings of the stone and the circuitry of what held it together.

Zelwa thought about Timon and suddenly felt unsure. She teetered on the edge of remembering that terrible day, but then veered off into a safer memory—her first memory of him. She impressed the images into the stone as she experienced it in her mind and felt the remembered emotions in her body. Feeling the emotions was the hardest part.

> *"He's so small," were my first words on seeing him. I whispered it as I looked down at him sleeping in his bassinet. I was six. My dad was standing with me. The birth had exhausted my*

mom, and she was resting. We already had several people to manage the house and to help with the baby for the first few months.

"His name is Timon," my father whispered. "You're a big sister now."

It was a magical moment, watching Timon sleeping, bundled up safely in his swaddling. I instantly fell in love with him and began making plans for all the fun things we would do together.

But being a big sister wasn't all fun and games. Zelwa let her thoughts flow to another memory.

I heard something fall in my room as I walked in and there was a three-year-old Timon, climbing my bookshelf, trying to reach one of my stuffed animals on the top shelf. The thing that fell was a clay chickadee I had made at school. It broke into several pieces on the floor.

"Timon!" I yelled. I was angry about the broken bird, but also annoyed that he was in my room and trying to get my things. The annoyance quickly turned to fear as he turned in alarm at the sound of his name and lost his footing. He

tumbled off the bookshelf, hitting the floor before I could get to him. Thankfully, unlike the bird, he didn't break. He stood up unfazed, laughed, and ran out of the room, leaving me to pick up my broken chickadee and put it in the trash.

My mom hired Lyda not long after that. Someone had to watch Timon and keep him entertained because the ways he entertained himself were often not safe. The older he got the more he seemed to want to get into.

"Too curious," Lyda would say with a smile. Her presence was good for Timon. But she wasn't always there.

That thought brought Zelwa back to the memory she was avoiding. She still felt a little unsure about delving into it, but now she was so close. Her own curiosity allowed her to relax slightly, pulling the memory forward and reliving it as she pushed the energy of it into that connection.

I stepped out of the school transport, waved goodbye to my friends as the door whooshed closed and the transport went about its route.

The warmth of the sun felt soothing. Bees and wasps zoomed by, enjoying the many flowers in the gardens surrounding the house. I smelled roses and sage. The growing area wasn't huge, but each house had enough for sustainability if needed. As I walked towards the doorway to our house, I was already thinking how nice it would be to get out of this stuffy school uniform and do some reading in the hammock. I made it to the door, pulling it open with a spirited tug.

"I'm hooommme!" I yelled into the living room.

Zelwa gulped. Until this point, the memory was pleasant. Happy even. She wasn't sure she wanted to go on. But she still wanted to know if Impressing the memory gave her any relief. This early in the memory, Zelwa felt carefree and even a bit silly. She'd heard a joke at school that she thought would make Timon laugh. When he wasn't being attention-grabbing and annoying, she loved making him smile and always spent the first moments home from school with him. Zelwa felt her connection with the stone flicker, so she focused again. She'd come this far, she might as well see it through.

The silence that followed my announcement wasn't normal. Timon should run up with one of his games or toys, followed by Lyda.

"Timon?" Nothing. "Lyda?" Still nothing. "Mom? Dad?"

I walked through the living room to the elevator. Our house only had one upper floor, but it went three floors underground. That is where Mom and Dad had their work areas, the labs. I pressed the intercom.

"I'm home."

After several moments.

"Zelwa?" My mother's voice.

"Yes. Where's Timon?"

"He should be with Lyda. Like usual."

"Lyda was off today," Dad's voice chimed in. "Weren't you going to take him to the museum, Annette?

Silence. Mom had forgotten, lost in her work. The house never seemed silent. Timon was always full of energy and laughter. It occurred to me that the silence was unnatural. I felt the first twinge of fear.

"I'm coming up," Mom said. Her voice was unreadable. "Zelwa, find your brother."

"What's happened? Is he missing?" Dad asked. "Annette?"

I heard the hum of the elevator machinery activate. Realizing that Timon had been left alone for hours, I began running through the rooms of the house and finding each one empty, my heart beating faster each time I turned a corner and he wasn't there. I was intentionally avoiding one area of the house. Timon wasn't supposed to go there unless someone was with him, but Timon had gotten away from Lyda a few times and it was where he usually ended up.

I was standing at the entryway to the small swimming pool, frozen in place, as my mother ran up behind me, as breathless as I was. My heart was pounding, but I felt chilled to the bone.

"I couldn't find him in the house," I whispered.

My mom was quiet, and I knew she was seeing the same thing that I saw - something floating in the water, unmoving.

Zelwa felt frozen in her Impressing the same way she felt frozen watching the swimming pool. She didn't know if she could go any further today. She wasn't ready. It suddenly seemed like a stupid idea. Zelwa broke the Impressing and pushed the memory back into the safety of her mind.

Zelwa looked up at Elder, waiting for his commentary, but Elder was watching Mora, who was still focused on her stone. Elder was frowning. Mora's face scrunched up in concentration. Sweat dribbled down the right side of her face. Part of the stone bulged. Elder stepped forward and touched Mora. Her connection to the stone broke.

"You've made more progress than expected," Elder said. "But you need to have more understanding before you try that again."

"What happened?"

Mora grinned.

"I think I can manipulate the stone."

"We'll begin a different practice tomorrow," Elder said. "And proceed safely." Elder turned to Zelwa. "You were doing well, but then stopped."

"Yes," Zelwa said. "The memory...I wasn't ready."

"Why did you choose that memory?" Elder asked. "I could sense your unease."

"It's not a good memory," Zelwa said. "I wanted to see if you were right. That maybe it would hurt less after an Impressing."

Elder nodded in understanding.

Zelwa saw Mora playing with the rocks on the table, picking them up and looking at each one, moving them around.

"Impressing doesn't resolve the emotions around a memory. What I meant before is that it could give you new perspective. If you come back to view it when you're not feeling what you felt in that moment, you might see it differently."

"May I go?" Mora asked.

"We need to talk about what you did," Elder said, turning to Mora.

"Can we do that later? I forgot I must help with food preparation."

Elder watched Mora for a few moments, but then nodded. As she walked out of the room, he turned back to Zelwa.

"What you've Impressed will remain there. You can complete it when you are ready."

Zelwa nodded. She wasn't sure if she wanted to complete it. Remembering it didn't change the result. To take her mind off the subject, she decided she would find Mora and ask about what she had done. It was odd that she had left so quickly. Usually, she had a thousand questions for Elder after they were done with a session. Also, neither of them was on the food prep roster.

"Thank you, Elder."

"Let me know if you require anything else. You are doing well."

Zelwa nodded, a little more slowly this time. She watched Elder take her rock and put it on the shelf. There were several rocks still on the table. Something didn't feel right there, but Zelwa thought maybe it was just the weirdness of what Mora had done. But then she realized what it was. Zelwa had counted eleven rocks on the table when they had come into the room earlier. She counted them again, taking into consideration that Elder had put hers and Mora's away. There were only eight left when there should have been nine. Mora had taken one.

CHAPTER 5: UNWELCOME SURPRISE
JAREM

Tock hid in the back room of a Mekla shop with two Earthers from the marketplace. The resurrects had floated through all force fields as if they didn't exist. He watched Rema dart off in a different direction. That was for the best. Groups of Earthers together were easier to hunt.

"Stay quiet," Tock whispered to the two trembling women. "If we survive this, I can get you to safety."

If...the word hung in the air.

They were quiet. One benefit of being in survival mode most of your life was that the instinct was strong. The three Earthers hunkered down like frightened prey, trying not to make a sound.

The resurrects had definitely taken victims. He'd heard the screams and the sound of ripping flesh as he led the Earthers he could away from the circle and in and out several shops before he found this room. They had slid behind several containers. He hoped it was enough. They waited and waited.

At some point, Tock heard footsteps in the store. He tensed. Resurrects didn't take footsteps, but any number of beings might think it amusing to toss them out to the resurrects or even try to keep them to sell them after the danger had passed. The steps grew closer. They sounded slow and methodical. Not a good sign.

Tock held his breath. The other Earthers did the same. Tock tilted his head between the containers, trying to see what might be coming for them. He was relieved to see Kin. He was about to call out her name when she turned to face their hiding place and he saw her eyes. The red glow within them grew brighter as they locked onto him and then there was darkness, the darkness of space. Something moved in the darkness, some enormous energetic body lying in the emptiness, tossing and turning as if in a dark nightmare.

It turned over once more and stilled. The eyes opened.

Jarem woke from his rest with a jolt. The dream of Tock felt more than a dream. He rolled over and sat up on his bunk. The craft they had rented was small, but had a shared area with ten beds in the walls. He saw Rema at a table, talking with the rescued Earther. As Jarem looked around, he saw Nelly bolt upright across the room, then Peet. They both looked over at Jarem.

"Did you dream it, too?"

Jarem nodded.

"We should have gone back to get him!" Nelly spat. "We should have never let them go!"

"It was your idea to save the Earthers," Peet said. "We could have all just left."

"Peet!" Rema turned and glared at her brother. Nelly did the same.

"What?" Peet said. "We had a clear mission. We broke protocol and now look at us. Look at what happened with Kin. What does a resurrect do with consciousness? We gave them the edge when we're supposed to be stopping them!"

Nelly slipped out of her bunk and took a couple of steps towards Peet, her fists balled up tight. Peet shifted as if about to leave his bunk as well. Jarem felt the tension. He felt the pain. He needed to divert the emotion into something more useful, if possible.

"Tock was my best friend," Jarem said. "My first real friend."

"Don't talk about him like that!" Nelly cried. "We don't know that he's dead. Maybe..."

Peet rubbed his hands over his eyes and face and shook his head. The anger and pain were still there for both him and Nelly, but the moment of distraction allowed for their training to kick in.

"This is irrational," Peet said. "I need some time to process it. And time is something that we don't really have."

He lay back down in his bunk and triggered the mechanism to close himself off.

Nelly was still angry, but Jarem could feel it beginning to shift to grief. He could see the tears forming and feel the emotion trying to push them out. Nelly looked at Jarem and Rema. She was attempting to control her breathing and struggling with it.

When she could speak, she said, "I need some time as well." She walked over and sat in a corner.

Jarem knew Nelly and Peet would come back when they were ready. Jarem wished he could take away Nelly's pain. She would need to work through it. They had all dealt with loss. But they had also grown accustomed to hope. He sent telepathic support to them both and trusted that they knew their way back. When they had more time, they would revisit it and see what further work needed to be done.

Jarem stood and walked over to Rema and the Earther she rescued.

"How is he?" Jarem asked.

"He's okay," Rema said. "But he's not an Earther."

"What?"

"I'm half Earther," the man said. "My name is Stavo."

"Half?"

"Yes. I keep getting passed around and sold for slaughter trials. And I keep surviving them. Eight so far. Resurrects only like the full-fledged Earthers, you know."

Slaughter trials. Jarem hated the name, but it was an appropriate description. Certain beings found it amusing to take humanoids that look like Earthers, mix them in with a group of Earthers and allow bets to be made on which ones were actual Earthers. They then monitored resurrect clusters and set up the would-be Earthers where the resurrects would find them to see who won—the Earthers, of course, never did.

"I'm guessing you've made beings like Sloctum a lot of money," Jarem couldn't keep some anger out of his voice.

"What would you have me do?" Stavo said. "You think I can just exist looking like this? If only I looked more like my father, I wouldn't have to survive in this way."

Interspecies relationships weren't unusual, but Jarem had heard too many times about Earthers being purchased as exotic pets or being kept as concubines. Jarem didn't dare ask. He could feel Stavo's anger.

Stavo had trauma, too, just different than typical Earthers. Stavo was resentful. Not fearful.

"We've all had to survive the best way we can," Rema said. She looked at Jarem. "He's here now."

"I am sorry you wasted your time on me," Stavo said. "And lost two of your friends."

Jarem felt his sincerity.

"You with us now," Jarem said. "At least you won't be sold for another slaughter trial."

Stavo sighed wearily. "For now."

"We really have nothing to show for what happened at Big Mek," Rema said. "Kin and Tock are gone. And all for nothing."

"We know it doesn't work that way. We're just not seeing it correctly," Jarem said. "We have to keep our minds focused. When we arrive at the coordinates, we may need to act quickly. Who knows what is there or what we'll need to do?"

Rema glanced over at Nelly in the corner and then Peet's closed bunk.

"We're definitely off track," Rema said. She sighed and dropped her head. When she looked up, Jarem could see she was crying. "I'm not okay, either. I'm trying to hold it together."

Jarem put his hand on Rema's shoulder. He knew this mission was going to take a toll on them, but they had barely gotten started and didn't know much about what would await them at their destination.

"We should all rest. Once we've had some time to process all that has happened, we can decide how to proceed."

Rema nodded wearily.

"You should rest, too, Stavo," Jarem said. "You're safe here."

Stavo grunted but stood and walked over to an open bed. "I'm usually safe," he said as he lay down. "It just hasn't gotten me very far other than staying alive."

Rema went to a bunk and lay down. Jarem went back to his. He looked around, noting that what remained of his team was separated by emotion and bunks. Nothing was going quite as planned. They all needed to grieve, and yet they all needed to be ready for whatever came next.

Jarem sat back in his bunk and tapped into the surrounding emotions and found himself focusing more on what was missing: Kin and Tock

One thing Jarem could always count on in times like this was Tock rallying everyone and getting them refocused. Jarem was a little envious of that. Sure, he could read emotions and even influence them a little, but it wasn't as authentic as what Tock did. Tock knew everyone by listening and watching. He picked up on things that Jarem didn't because Jarem didn't need to. Jarem could feel if someone was upset or happy or whatever; he could even pick up on certain thoughts if they were strong enough. Tock could tell by looking at someone that they needed comforting. He paid attention to his friends and offered whatever they needed. If he had been there, he probably would have brought them all in for a big group hug.

Jarem thought about the first time he and Tock had met. The Yacca couldn't buy every Earther that ended up on the selling block on Hanu without causing conflict. Instead, they purchased them from other locations. Many of the first Earthers the Yacca took in were so traumatized that they kept to themselves or tried to escape. The Yacca didn't stop them. There were also many that realized that it was probably safer to stay with the Yacca than it was to be on the run. At least they had access to food and water.

From his very arrival, Tock was full of hope even though he was alone and young, like Jarem. Jarem became his friend partly out of curiosity and partly because Tock wouldn't have it any other way. Tock's hopefulness was infectious, and Jarem felt it healing him. That was where the idea started to begin a process to help the new Earthers that were arriving on Hanu process their traumatic experiences and find new purpose. It wasn't an easy process. None of them had a lot of experience in having a purpose or expecting anything more out of life than being on the run and occasionally finding some food that wasn't already halfway rotten.

It was Tock's idea to form a team to go out and rescue Earthers from places that the Yacca didn't know to look because they had never been on the run and didn't know the hiding places that Earthers like Jarem and Tock had been born and raised in.

In the beginning, it was just him and Tock. Jarem stumbled onto the idea of remote viewing through books the Yacca had procured for them about their species' history. It opened a whole new way of finding Earthers. At first it was just Jarem remote viewing. Then they found Nelly and Rema and Peet. Nelly was the toughest find. She had been protecting two Earthers younger than her and had attacked them when she realized they were following her. Once she realized they were Earther, too, that all changed. When they found Kin, it felt like the unit was complete. All the other Earthers became a part of the civilization they were creating inside Hanu.

Jarem felt the overall emotions of the ship level out a bit. Now he was ready to do some work. He closed off his bunk. A dim light came on above Jarem. He turned it off so that he was in complete darkness. He didn't want any distractions.

Jarem slowed his breathing and relaxed his body until he felt weightless. He focused on the target in his mind.

The coordinates he concentrated on were the ones identified when he and his team remote viewed to find an answer to the resurrect problem. They had used the remote viewing process prior to that to find Earthers to rescue and supplies that would be of use to Earthers. They had so much success that one day it seemed the most natural course to use it to find a way to stop the resurrects altogether.

As Jarem drifted in the trance, he allowed his senses to explore the coordinates, trying to get an idea of what they might find when they arrived. He suddenly felt cold and a feeling of darkness, like endless space. An image appeared in his mind of a thread, or some thin cord stretched to near breaking.

It wasn't very encouraging. He knew the coordinates were on a planet and not in space. He continued to be open to whatever other information he could receive. The pressure of bringing everyone back together crept into the trance. He wasn't sure he was up to it. He wasn't sure that he hadn't been a coward to leave Tock and Kin behind.

Jarem's mouth dried out and tasted like dust. He felt everything was falling apart around him. A ripple of fear passed through his body. He tried to stop it, but he felt it passing out of him and then circling back, stronger than before. It continued to build. Jarem twisted in his bunk, trying to gain control. He tried to break his trance, knowing he hadn't gotten anything of substance to act on.

As he fought to open his eyes, his mind was filled with screams.

CHAPTER 6: SOMETHING NEW
ZELWA

"What are you doing?"

Mora jumped and looked up at Zelwa. Zelwa had followed her from the cave and off-trail on the planet to a spot where Mora could hide from anyone else. Zelwa had lost her for a bit, so she climbed up on some large stones, walking around and looking for Mora. She found her in a little alcove. Zelwa spoke to her from above.

"Go away, Zelwa."

"It's not safe for you to practice without Elder," Zelwa said. She began making her way down to Mora.

"That's what he says," Mora said. "I'm not doing anything dangerous. I think I'm close to something. It would be fun to figure it out and show him."

"Mora..."

"Don't be so by-the-book," Mora said.

"What's that supposed to mean?"

"Nothing," Mora said, then sighed. "Well, if you must know, you're a lot like your mother. Always work and no play."

"That's not true," Zelwa said. "I just like to keep to myself." The last thing she wanted to be was like her mother. She also didn't have much she felt she could talk about with someone else.

"I like to keep to myself, too," Mora said. "If you don't mind, you can go now."

"I'll have to tell Elder."

"Why not just tell your mother? Of course you'd tell. But why? We could discover something that will be beneficial to everyone."

"Elder says there are rules and you have to be careful. We promised to follow his rules. That's the only reason he allowed us here. Rules keep us safe."

"I've Impressed about a dozen times now. I want to do more. I know I can do more."

"What were you doing in the training today? I saw the stone bulge."

"See? You are curious, too. Come here," Mora said.

"This doesn't mean that I'm going to help you," Zelwa said. But she was curious, and that stopped her for a moment. Was curiosity something she wanted to indulge? Timon was curious about the swimming pool—always wanting to go there, not waiting for an adult to take him, not understanding the risks. He thought the safety he felt floating around with adults would still be there when he was alone. "I don't know, Mora."

"Just watch," Mora said. "I'll do this one quick thing and I'll take the rock back. Okay?"

"You promise?" Zelwa asked.

Mora nodded. Zelwa was still apprehensive, but she walked over, thinking that she could always stop Mora if she needed to.

"Great!" Mora smiled. "So, I felt something in the connection when I was working the stone and I wonder if it is what Elder feels when he is making big changes with the minerals, like making the caverns. We know he communicates with something in the make-up of the stone. I think I sensed it. Maybe it's like Artificial Intelligence, except is it artificial if it is in a natural substance?"

Zelwa shrugged, not knowing what to say. Mora continued.

"The intelligence that we are using to encode our memories...well, I think that is the starting place to make a request and then it complies. I think I can do the same thing. I almost did it in class."

"Intelligence? Like something energetic in the stone?"

"I don't know what it is. It doesn't seem to have feelings. It just exists and shifts into different forms. I'm going to try something to see if I can get it to do what I ask."

"Mora, please be careful."

"Of course I'll be careful."

Mora placed the rock down and focused as Elder had taught them.

"The rocks that Elder gives us to use...He has primed them in some way to make it easier for us. Otherwise, I think we could Impress into any stone once we understand what is happening."

"What are you going to ask it to do?"

"I don't know," Mora said. "Maybe I'll have it shift into a stature of your mother." She snickered. "Would you be able to tell it from your actual mother?"

Zelwa scowled even though she was a little amused at comparing her mother to a statue.

"Okay, okay," Mora said. "I don't know. I have a feeling there is an energy source to be tapped into. Maybe we can get the ship powered up again."

Zelwa had to admit that she was intrigued by the idea.

"Don't overdo it," Zelwa said. "If you want to try a small experiment, fine. Just do it so we can get the rock back before Elder notices it is gone."

"You're the one holding me up," Mora said. "Sit over there. And don't interrupt."

Zelwa sat on a nearby rock and watched. Impressing could take a while, and Mora was doing something more complicated than that. She settled in, wondering what she had gotten herself into by looking for and finding Mora. She wouldn't have felt right knowing and not doing anything about it. Maybe she should have just said something to Elder and let him deal with it. But she hadn't been completely sure if Mora had taken it and thought maybe she could stop Mora before Mora got in trouble. That hadn't worked out the way she planned. At least she was here. Of course, if something went wrong, she wasn't sure what she should do. And, it was odd that Elder hadn't noticed that the stone was gone.

After several minutes of looking at the surrounding rocks, Zelwa wondered if she should just leave. Mora obviously didn't want her around. She waited. What else did she have to do?

Zelwa thought about what Mora had said about her being like her mother. Sure, she liked to follow the rules, but she wasn't like her mother. Her mother wouldn't have come looking for Mora. And Zelwa would never have forgotten about her brother if she had been at home that day.

Comparing her to her mom had been a mean thing to say. Maybe Mora wasn't the friend that Zelwa thought she was. And maybe she was someone that Zelwa shouldn't be hanging out with. But who else did Zelwa have to talk to? Sometimes it felt like interacting with other people was too much. Or maybe it was that she cared too much and didn't get anything back for her efforts. Maybe her mother loved Timon more than she loved Zelwa. Maybe Zelwa didn't really have a place in this world.

Before her thoughts could spiral even further down, a glow in the rock caught her attention. Mora was smiling. It didn't feel right. Zelwa could feel a wild, energetic buzz in the air. Zelwa stood and moved forward, wondering why she ever thought she could do anything to help Mora if things went wrong. The hairs on her arms and neck stood up on end. She was afraid to speak, afraid she would throw Mora off in a way that could cause an explosion or any other number of bad things, but she was also certain something bad was about to happen.

The glow in the stone shifted to the flat surface rock below it and ran forward several feet, then a pillar of stone grew out of the ground. Another grew nearby and they both extended several feet in the air and bent to meet each other, creating an arch.

Zelwa noticed that Mora's nose was bleeding and red ooze was slipping out of her ears. She rushed over and tried to shake Mora from behind, but Mora remained focused, as if in a trance. Zelwa jumped in front of her, tried to shake her again, anything to get her eyes to unlock from the rock.

The arch completed itself behind Zelwa as she shook Mora.

"I. Can't. Let. Go." Mora said, each word a massive effort.

"What is that?" Zelwa said, turning to take a look at the arch behind her.

"I. Can't. Hold. It. In."

The flash of light in the stone Mora was holding began pulsating faster and faster.

"Get. Elder."

Zelwa was still kneeling in front of Mora. There was no way she would get Elder in time to stop whatever was happening. Zelwa reached out to grab the stone and as her fingers grazed the stone's surface, Mora convulsed, her eyes rolling back into her head. The boulder underneath Zelwa trembled and the light coming from the rock glowed brighter and brighter until it exploded in a force that knocked Zelwa towards the arch. Zelwa fell backwards. She saw the top of the arch as the rock shifted and her feet lost the ground. She braced herself for the impact of landing on her back. As she fell, the light enveloped her, pulsing and pulsing, and then there was nothing.

CHAPTER 7: LOOKING FOR SOMETHING
JAREM

Jarem walked onto the spacecraft's bridge to find Dr. Yac sitting in meditation in the middle of the room. The spacecraft's navigation had been set for the coordinates his team had arrived at through remote viewings. He was still shaken from his recent attempt to gain information that way and had needed to remove himself from the emotions of the rest of the team to get clear. Jarem sat in a chair near Dr. Yac and closed his eyes, trying to regain a calm mind.

Not much longer.

Jarem opened his eyes and met those of Dr. Yac.

You are distracted.

"This isn't how I thought it would be," Jarem said.

"Is it ever?" Dr. Yac said aloud. "Each rescue mission you've been on, there have been circumstances that were unexpected."

"The stakes are higher for this mission," Jarem said. "And we've never encountered resurrects. I'm not even sure how that happened. Do you think they somehow have a sense about what we're doing? What we're trying to do?"

"No being has communicated with the resurrects. There have been no indications that they have any sort of awareness other than being able to identify Earthers and take them over. Until back at the portal, of course. That was surprising. I am sorry for the loss of your friend."

"Friends," Jarem said with a heavy heart. "I dreamed of Tock. I'm certain they have him as well."

Dr. Yac bowed his head, acknowledging Jarem's emotional pain.

"You should take time to be with your grief."

"There's no time," Jarem said. "I have to be focused on what is ahead. The window of opportunity is small." Jarem sighed, feeling helpless.

"You have changed so much since my Yacca clan found you. And yet you still carry a significant burden."

"I'm not sure I have much choice in that."

Dr. Yac watched Jarem for a few moments.

"You have chosen this path. And you are committed to it."

Jarem shifted uncomfortably in the seat. He *was* committed, but he was still unsure and scared.

"Do you remember the day you came to us?"

Jarem nodded.

"I do as well, though I was not at the portal station that day," Dr. Yac said. "We had watched many of your kind come and go in Mekla. The capture and selling of other creatures is not something we condone, but we are bound by portal station law. Also, it occurred to us that the situation must be happening because your species was balancing out an energetic debt. But then you asked us for help. And we heard you."

The words brought back the day for Jarem. By chance, the first time Jarem had reached out psychically to another being, it happened to be the Yacca. They heard his hope and his despair and did not leave him to the fate others were creating for him.

"When we heard you, we knew a major shift for your species had begun. And since you asked, we could answer."

"I know, and I'm grateful," Jarem said. Being accepted and helped by the Yacca was the only thing that had gotten them to where they were. He knew he never wanted to feel so helpless again and because he put everything into motion, he felt the weight of getting it right.

"What I mean to say is that since you asked, we could help you in some small ways along your journey. However, just because it was *you* that asked does not mean *you* have to claim responsibility for all things related to your kind. Your choice to reach out to us that day was a great life purpose. Even if your energy moves out of that body tomorrow or within the next few minutes, that act alone made your life valuable in a way that is greater than your single life."

Jarem contemplated the words. He knew logically that Dr. Yac was right, but he also still felt responsible, regardless.

"It is the same for the friends you lost. They lived according to their own choices and dedicated their lives to something greater than themselves. I only say these things to offer a way to shift the emotion around the current situation. I may have said too much and apologize. "

"I appreciate your words," Jarem said. "It feels like we have had so many successes in the past that the loss and the quickness of how it could happen was never in our minds."

Jarem and Dr. Yac sat in silence for several moments, as it felt nothing more needed to be said. Still wondering how to move forward in the best way, Jarem had an idea to get his mind oriented on the goal at hand.

"Could we practice?"

"Are you certain that is what you want?"

"Yes," Jarem said. The idea of preparing was much more appealing than wallowing in the trauma.

Jarem closed his eyes and waited. He hadn't practiced psychic defense with Dr. Yac, but he knew from the sessions he'd had with other Yacca that they liked to push him and to be clever in the attacks. Several moments passed and Jarem thought that Dr. Yac had decided not to take part when he felt it—the tiny pinprick in his consciousness of something that did not originate from him.

This was the danger in being out with beings that were more advanced in telepathy than most humans—they could manipulate you without you even realizing. Somehow, the humans that they were rescuing were more and more open to learning to develop their psychic abilities. They found that after much healing had taken place, they were all able to train to varying degrees to control their minds and not allow anyone to take advantage of them.

Jarem was adept at it. His gift had been what attracted the Yacca to them. Jarem and his friends had determined that it would be a good idea for Earth humans to defend themselves, even on the friendly planet of Hanu. The Yacca didn't interfere and even brought them guides and images and video from Earth to help them in learning martial arts. Jarem wasn't sure that it would help in dealing with the resurrects, but if any other species tried to enslave them again, they would not go easily.

Jarem closed off the tickle forming inside his mind. Tickle was the best way he could describe it, but its overall sensation was one of sedation—it felt like the tendril of something inching its way in to take over. Jarem felt it again, lighter, but still probing. He actually felt a sense of wanting to give up and just rest for a bit. That was always a sign of a powerful attack. Jarem reached into his memories and pulled forth the one that always brought him back to awareness, to his purpose:

And there was his mother's face and his most painful— and loving - memory. Her face filled his vision as she pressed her forehead to his.

"I love you. I will always love you." Jarem was crying and so was she, their tears mingling on Jarem's cheeks. "You must be quiet. You must survive."

Jarem wanted to protest, but they heard something coming. Jarem instinctively went quiet. His mom kissed him one last time on his forehead.

He didn't go further into the memory. He didn't need to. The tickle stopped and Jarem felt himself returning to a normal thought process.

Good, Dr. Yac sent to Jarem. *You are doing very well. Would you like to try on me?*

Jarem had only tried to infiltrate a Yacca on a few occasions and only with their permission. Delving into their mind was like taking a swim in the universe's vastness. Jarem didn't even know where to begin, but he had to appreciate that about the Yacca. They weren't just training him to protect himself as merely defensive and they didn't seem afraid of teaching him how to take the fight to another being–they didn't teach to harm, but to stop any further harm being done.

Jarem nodded and began the process. He felt his way into Dr. Yac's mind. He felt the vastness. He focused, thinking that there must be a way to control the Yacca. His intuition guided him to the planet Hanu in his mind. He focused further there, sending relaxing energy to the Yacca. He sensed something from Dr. Yac. *Amusement*! But, Jarem did not give up. He felt he was on to something. Maybe part of mind control was knowing your target. Sure, sending emotions could help in many cases, but only on beings with a low level of telepathy. On something like the Yacca, who could swat away his abilities like a small fly... Well, it had to be more personal.

Jarem thought more about Hanu and this Yacca, trying to sift through anything that would give him a memory to work with. He had seen Yacca resting before. Jarem also noted that Yacca have personalities and likes and dislikes. He realized that Dr. Yac liked to figure things out, take them a part, learn what makes them tick. Using that, Jarem reached in further and created a project in his mind, something that he had seen in one of the Earth books brought back to him by the Yacca. It was a game, a toy that Earth children once played with. Jarem had seen pictures and videos. He fed an image of this toy to the Yacca, trying to force the thought of curiosity. The small wooden doll opened up, and there was another inside. That one opened and there was another. And on and on. Jarem felt a release of something for a moment before Dr. Yac regained control and locked down tight on his mind.

Nice idea, Dr. Yac said. He was even smiling. *You learn quickly. I wasn't expecting you to try such a maneuver. You weren't successful, but it shows that you are developing an understanding.*

Jarem acknowledged the compliment with a nod.

And maybe one day I will get an opportunity to look at this item of amusement you projected to me.

The navigation showed the nearing of the destination. The ship's wall went transparent to show outside the ship. In all the vastness of space, Jarem and his team had been led to this destination. Jarem leaned in, watching the small planet grow in size as they approached.

"We're here," Jarem said, feeling the weight of the moment. So much depended on whatever was going to happen next.

"Yes," Dr. Yak said. "We have arrived at the planet called Laris."

"I'll prepare the others."

Jarem walked back into the living area. He wanted to see them and get a feel for how everyone was doing. The mood of the room was glum. It wasn't the excitement that he thought he would feel as they approached the coordinates that projected so much possibility.

"We've made it," Jarem said.

One by one, they nodded and stood and walked with Jarem to the bridge. All but Stavo. Jarem didn't feel any ill will from Stavo, so he let him be. They would let Stavo go at the first opportunity.

"The planet is desolate," Dr. Yak was saying as they entered and sat down. "I detect no life, though the atmosphere is conducive to it."

The team looked at one another quizzically.

"Hopefully, there is something there," Nelly said.

Dr. Yak landed the craft in a somewhat flattened area. Most of the planet was dry, with large rock clusters and hills.

"You'll have to walk to the coordinates," Dr. Yak said. "This is as close as we can land."

Jarem turned to what remained of his crew.

"I know this isn't how we wanted to go. The coordinates came through our team. We came as six because we don't know what we'll find and we wanted the opportunity to go deeper again. We still don't know what we will find. But we're here. We have produced actionable intel over and over. Something is here, some clue to stop the resurrects. We just have to find it."

Jarem didn't ask how they were feeling. He could feel it already. They were disheartened about the loss of Kin and Tock, but there was hope there, too. They had all lived through enough loss to know that there were times to hunker down and times to keep moving. Moving meant you were alive. It meant you had a chance to survive.

"Let's find it," Rema said.

"I hope whatever it is, however we end them...I hope it hurts," Nelly said. She was emanating anger. Jarem would take that. Anger could make you careless, but sometimes it kept you going when you needed to go.

"For Tock and Kin," Peet said.

"For Tock and Kin," Jarem said quietly. "And all the others before them."

A moment of silence passed to acknowledge the loss.

"I'll lead the way," Nelly said as she opened the door and began walking down the ramp to the planet.

Despite being dry and having no plant life, the planet had enough oxygen for them to breathe without an aura field.

Nelly led them through paths between the rocks and over boulders until they came to a small opening in the rocks. In the center was a stone arch.

"That doesn't fit anything else here," Peet said. The arch was smooth and the precision of the curve was unnatural. "Someone made that."

"Dr. Yak said there isn't any life here," Rema said.

Jarem walked over and reached out to touch the arch.

"Wait!" Nelly said. "We don't know what will happen."

"We came all this way," Jarem said. "This is the spot. I'm not leaving until we learn what we need to know." As he finished speaking, he placed his palm on the arch. Nothing happened. Jarem walked all around it, looking for anything that might activate it or indicate why they should be there.

"What if the resurrects came out of that?" Peet said. "Maybe we don't want to make it do anything. More resurrects could come out. Maybe we have to destroy it."

"Perhaps," Jarem said. "We don't have enough information. I wouldn't want to destroy it before we know for sure."

Jarem didn't want to say it, but this process would be so much easier if they had all six of them here. But wishing wasn't going to make it happen.

"Let's think back to the remote viewing. We were focused on discovering something that would stop the resurrects. Now we are here. The time is right. Let's run through the visuals again."

They spent the next several moments going through everything they felt, imagined, whatever, during the remote viewing. Nothing was clear.

"We can't leave until we find out. We can't. Something has to be here," Jarem said.

"You should contact Dr. Yak. He might have some ideas." That was Nelly.

Jarem connected telepathically with Dr. Yak.

How are things?

We found a stone arch, but don't know what to do now. We don't want to leave, however, because we're within the window of time and don't want to miss anything.

Then wait. All appears to be safe.

Jarem and his team sat around the arch. Peet pulled a container of dried berries out of his pack and offered it to the group.

"We could talk about Kin and Tock," Jarem said. "But only if you want to. We always know there is the possibility for us to die or...be taken. I didn't think it would be today. I wasn't prepared for that."

Nelly looked down. Peet picked a piece of berry out of his teeth.

"Kin wasn't just my friend," Rema said. "We were thinking of making an official union."

Nelly looked up at Rema.

"I didn't know that," she said.

"I knew about you and Tock," Rema said. "I saw you two kissing."

Nelly blushed.

"We need to make some decisions about how long we should wait and if there are other options," Peet interjected.

"We-"

The arch lit up.

"Something is happening..."

"We can see that..."

"Everyone take cover!"

The group scattered around the clearing, bracing themselves behind boulders. Jarem peered around his boulder, watching as the glow of the arch increased in intensity until a massive pulse of energy emanated from it. Jarem ducked back behind the boulder for protection.

Jarem took one last peek as the pulse intensified. He could see something coming through the light. As he squinted to make out what it was, he thought he could see the silhouette of something against the brightness. Someone or something was coming.

CHAPTER 8: THE SWIRLING
ZELWA

I'm dreaming, Zelwa thought. *I must be dreaming.*

The words drifted away as she tried to focus on their meaning. Her mind was a fog of memory snippets floating in and out of her consciousness, spinning around her like a kaleidoscope.

Where am I?

Could she be asleep? Zelwa tried to move her fingers, toes - anything. She couldn't feel her body at all and had the sensation that she was stretched across space.

How would that even be possible? I must be having some sort of out-of-body experience.

Zelwa remembered reading about those. They had a couple of people with the expedition that regularly had them. Zelwa had never felt the need to try. She tried to move again, but just hovered in the same space. It seemed like time had possibly passed, but the pulses of memory around her were slowing down, staying longer. She reached out for one as an anchor point.

Mora flashed in her mind. Then came the memory of Mora and the stone and Zelwa being flung backwards. Zelwa released the memory with a jolt to her awareness.

I must be dreaming.

The word dreaming made her think of the word drowning. And she did feel like she was drowning, but that connection made her think of Timon and the memory rolled by in slow motion—every detail preserved.

Her thoughts were still hard to hold onto, but she was also feeling her awareness becoming stronger, almost as if the scattered parts of herself were being magnetized back to her...soul? Zelwa hadn't decided about how all the spiritual stuff worked.

I just have to wake up.

Zelwa tried to open her eyes and couldn't figure out how to do so. She again attempted to move her arms and legs. It felt as though her body didn't exist, yet she felt the essence of herself moving.

I feel something warm.

It was a strange thought because she didn't really feel anything. It was another thing to latch onto.

Something warm.

Zelwa had a sense of light even though she couldn't discern where her eyes or eyelids were. The sensation was peculiar, but thinking of light caused another memory to float by. It was Mora again - Mora and the pulsating light. She wondered where Mora was and if she had hit her head when she fell.

Zelwa tried to reach for her head and her thoughts drifted again as she couldn't feel her hands - or arms, or head.

Mora.

Mora's face lingered and she felt anger and sadness. Why hadn't Mora listened to Elder? Why would she try something so dangerous? Then she felt worried. Was Mora hurt?

Mora?

Zelwa didn't have a voice. She remembered falling backwards, but not hitting anything.

Am I dead?

That didn't seem right. Of course, she had never died before, so why should she expect to know what it was like? The idea made her uneasy. And scared. She felt incredibly alone and unsure what to do.

Zelwa had a sudden feeling of searching for something, reaching out, trying to find something that was missing. How would she find something when nothing in her current state seemed tangible?

She had the sense of holding onto a single thread, a lifeline to her memories and feelings and she was only getting drips from it, but she knew she needed to hang on. It was all she had.

The images around her swirled again as she tried to make sense of what was happening to her. She thought of her mom and dad. If she was unconscious, would they have found her? Could she be in a coma?

Mom? Dad? Please help me!

The floating images stopped around her.

"Mom? Dad?"

Zelwa realized she had the sensation of hearing her voice. She looked down and saw her body. She still couldn't feel it, but she moved the image of her hands and they moved. As she glanced down at her feet, the surrounding area became a familiar place—a park near their home on Earth. The trees were fully green around a picnic area. Zelwa wasn't wearing shoes, and she squeezed her toes into the dirt and grass. She couldn't feel it, but the sight made her smile.

"There you are," a voice said.

Zelwa looked up and saw her dad walking towards her. Behind him was her mother. Something didn't seem right. They were wearing normal clothes, not their typical work clothes.

And they were smiling.

"What's going on?" Zelwa asked, taking a step backward as her dad approached.

He stopped. Her mom walked up to stand beside him. They looked at each other, but were no longer smiling. They seemed concerned.

"Zelwa," her mom began, "I--"

"Where are we? How did we get here?" Zelwa asked, still keeping her distance. "Is this real? I can't feel anything."

Zelwa sensed her awareness losing its grip on the moment, and the scene flickered. Her mom and dad stepped forward, grabbing her. It was a strange sensation. Zelwa still couldn't feel her body, but she felt something when her parents touched her– something other than her awareness. The park came back into view.

"Stay with us for a bit," her father said.

"We've missed you," her mother said.

"Is this some sort of trick?" Zelwa asked. She looked from her mom to her dad. They were still holding her and smiling. It was unnerving.

"Don't be afraid," her mother said, then laughed. "Sorry. I don't mean to tell you what to do. Old habits."

She reached over and grabbed her husband's hand. "I mean to say you are safe here."

"What is here?" Zelwa asked slowly.

"It's not so much a place," Zelwa's dad said. He looked at Zelwa's mom. "But we wanted to be here with you. We realize we haven't always been there with you." For a moment, her dad's smile faltered.

Zelwa felt something. If they hadn't still held her, she thought she might be flung backwards from the shock of the words in the same way she had been flung away from Mora. She could feel their presence giving her stability. Maybe she was having one of those dreams where you worked out your real-life problems. Zelwa didn't know how to respond to it all.

"Let's sit and talk," Zelwa's mom said. She pointed to a picnic table that hadn't been there a moment ago but appeared as she gestured towards it.

This definitely is a dream, Zelwa thought. *Or my mom has become a magician!*

Zelwa smiled to herself at the ridiculousness of the idea. She let herself be led to the table, and they all sat down. Zelwa wondered how she could sit without feeling anything, but allowed the dream to distract

105

her. Her parents kept their hands on her, and it was soothing, but also disconcerting. What would her psyche lead her to with her parents?

"So....," Zelwa began. "What brings you here? And, if you know, what brings me here? And could you also tell me what is happening?"

"We don't have all the answers. You called us. We came," her mother said. "We love you. We want to make sure you know that. I have not been great at showing you that."

"Yes, Zelwa," her father said. "Please know that we love you."

This dream is getting so weird. They would never say that. Especially not Mom!

Zelwa felt antsy. She wasn't sure she was ready for this conversation. She was still angry at her mom for ignoring her for months. Her dad hadn't been much better. That reminded Zelwa of another sore spot. Something was missing in this psychosomatic dream trip. The missing piece to the puzzle.

"Where's Timon?" Zelwa asked. "This dream should definitely have Timon in it."

Her parents looked at one another.

"He had something he needed to do," Zelwa's mother said.

"He was too busy for my dream?" Zelwa grinned. "He must be around here somewhere."

Zelwa pulled her hands free from her parents and stood.

"Zelwa, wait," her mother said.

Zelwa didn't respond. She could hear running water nearby, a creek meandering through the woods.

"I bet I know where he is," Zelwa said, walking away from her parents and towards the sound of water. The thought of seeing Timon again made her smile as she increased her pace.

"Zelwa, please wait," said her father's voice, but it sounded much further away than it should have.

Zelwa struggled to hold on to the image of the forest. It was harder without her parents touching her. She ran towards the creek, strangely sure that Timon would be there.

But he wasn't. No one was at the creek. The water flowed through the forest and as Zelwa watched it, it turned to light—a flowing stream of light running through the vastness of a night sky. Zelwa had the sudden fear that he was in the stream already. She waded in, looking for any sign of something under the light.

She didn't see him, but the warmth was returning. She wondered if her parents would appear again, but they didn't. Instead, she felt a heaviness growing around her awareness. It grew and grew until she felt she was falling from the weight of herself.

She had the smallest clarity of mind to brace herself as she fell and fell, waiting for impact.

CHAPTER 9: SOMEONE NEW

JAREM

Jarem could feel adrenaline running through his system as the silhouette of a person tumbled out of the arch and fell to the ground with a thump. He could feel the anxiousness in his team. They were all ready to bolt at the first sign of trouble. The energy pulse subsided. Jarem could hear the groans of the person on the ground, a girl, probably close in age to his team. He felt a wave of caution pass to him from his team and he took note, waiting to see what unfolded before he made his presence known.

He positioned himself between two rocks and shifted quietly to look through the crack between them.

The girl had landed on her back in a puff of dust. He watched as she turned on her side, coughed a few times, and then looked around her. Her face scrunched up in confusion.

"Mora?"

She pushed herself up, dusting off her gray uniform. She looked like an Earther.

"Mom? Dad?"

The girl stepped closer to the arch and reached out to touch it and seemed surprised by the contact. She stamped her feet on the ground and then spent several moments touching her head, face, and arms. She then looked around the area again, squinting her eyes and pursing her lips.

"Mora," she said with determination, and darted off down a path out of the opening.

Jarem and his team popped out from their hiding spaces.

"We can't lose her," Nelly whispered.

THE RESURRECTION INCIDENT

Jarem nodded, and they followed. Jarem hadn't gotten a read on the girl, so he had to hurry to keep her in sight as she made her way. He couldn't feel her presence as he could with most other beings. Either she was very focused on where she was going or never suspected someone was following her because she never looked back. She finally arrived at what looked like a large rocky hill amongst the boulders.

Jarem and his team watched as she walked up to the hill and touched it, appearing confused. She then began walking around it and disappeared. They hurried to follow and found an entrance inside the hill. Inside was a spacecraft, much bigger than what they had come in. The loading dock was open. Strangely, the ship hadn't registered when Dr. Yac scanned the planet.

"I'll go in and find her," Jarem said.

"We should stick together," Nelly said. "I don't…"

"We don't have time and I don't want to frighten her," Jarem said.

"Could you tell if she's friend or foe?" Rema asked.

"I didn't get anything from her yet," Jarem said. "I'm going in. This is my part."

"We'll wait for a bit, but then we will come in and find you," Nelly said.

"Let Dr. Yac know what we've found," Jarem said to Peet. "Maybe he can figure out why it didn't show up in the scan."

Peet nodded and began tapping on his wrist comms.

Jarem walked up the ramp and into the ship. It was powered up and humming. The ship appeared to be going through a cleaning cycle as dust was being blown up into the air and then sucked out through the ventilation. It looked like maybe it had been sitting unused for a while.

Jarem wasn't sure what direction the girl had gone, so he walked slowly, tentatively, down one of the large corridors. It startled him when she popped out of one of the side rooms. They both jumped in surprise.

"Who are you?" the girl asked.

Jarem wasn't ready to tell her everything just yet, so he said, "My name is Jarem. And you?"

"I'm Zelwa, " she said slowly. "You didn't arrive with us."

Zelwa looked at him skeptically, but Jarem noticed that he still wasn't getting any feeling or emotion from her.

"I only just arrived," Jarem said.

"Are you real?"

"What do you mean by...?" Before he could finish, Zelwa walked over and pinched his left shoulder. "Ow!"

"Sorry," Zelwa said. "I was just making sure."

"Do you encounter a lot of beings that aren't really here?" Jarem asked, rubbing his shoulder.

Zelwa didn't answer. She just looked at him, but then her eyes lit up.

"Did you come from Earth?" she asked. "Did our message finally get through?"

Jarem hesitated. From Earth? Could she not know? He wasn't sure how much he should tell her.

"I am an Earther."

"An Earther?" Zelwa smirked. "That's a weird thing to say. Do you mean from Earth? So am I. Where is everyone? At the cave?"

"I have seen no one other than you. Are there others?"

"That's strange," Zelwa touched her head. Again, Jarem couldn't feel anything from her, but she appeared to be confused. "It looks like they moved out everything, so they must be at the cave, but..."

"What is it?"

"We still had a week's worth of moving to do when I was last here."

"When was that?"

"This morning."

Zelwa walked past Jarem and down the corridor to another area of the ship. Jarem followed. It was some sort of eating area.

"The ship seems nearly fully powered up, but it was failing before..."

"There was a pulse of energy earlier," Jarem said. He didn't want to tell her yet that he had seen her come out of the arch. She didn't react.

Zelwa accessed a computer there, checking data.

"That's not possible."

"What's wrong?"

"The log shows the ship was powered down."

"It appears that was the case."

"But the timestamp..."

"What about it?"

"It shows that it only just powered back up."

"Right. The energy pulse?"

"Maybe. But it calibrated that the ship has been powered down for over 300 years." Zelwa frowned. "That's ridiculous." She looked at Jarem. "Isn't it?"

"I don't know," Jarem said. "What about the caves? Is it possible that someone is still there?" Jarem didn't want to tell her that the planet showed no life. But, they also hadn't picked up on this abandoned ship's presence.

Zelwa gave Jarem a long, hard look.

"Who are you again? And why are you here?"

"I understand your concern," Jarem said. "We should talk." Jarem sent her reassurance but could not see that it had any effect. "I should tell you I'm not alone."

Zelwa shifted on her feet, backing away from Jarem.

"Did you do something to my family?"

"No," Jarem said. "Of course not."

"Then why are you here?"

"My team and I came here to find something."

"What? We don't have anything. We're just a group of explorers."

"We don't know exactly. Perhaps you could help us. You're the only person we've encountered since we landed."

Zelwa watched Jarem for several moments. At least by now, Jarem was certain she wasn't a resurrect. And she didn't seem to have any ill intent.

"Where are the others?"

"Just outside," Jarem said. "We can go to them. I promise we mean you no harm." Jarem tried to send her assurance again and, again, it seemed to have no effect.

"How many of you are there?"

"Three more Earthers, a half-Earther, and a Yacca. Just the three Earthers are outside. Would you like to meet them?"

Zelwa frowned and Jarem wasn't sure if she was going to trust him, but then she smiled and said, "Sure. Maybe we can figure this out together." Jarem still couldn't get a read on her. The smile seemed forced.

Jarem and Zelwa walked to the ship entrance. Peet, Rema, and Nelly were nowhere to be seen, but then Jarem felt them.

"It's okay. You can come out."

Slowly, the three Earthers slipped out from behind rocks. Jarem introduced his crew to Zelwa and Zelwa to them. They all eyed one another. Jarem could feel wariness coming from his friends, but still nothing from Zelwa. He almost pinched her shoulder to make sure she was really there.

The halfling has left the ship.

The message came from Dr. Yak to Jarem.

"I think Stavo is trying to escape," Jarem sighed.

"He's not our captive. Besides, where is he going to go?" Nelly asked. She was eyeing Zelwa pretty hard, and Jarem was worried that she might jump her at any moment. Jarem tried to reassure her.

"What direction is he heading?" Rema asked her comms. She looked at the group. "We can't just let him wander around aimlessly."

"He is near you all, but he may not cross your path," Dr. Yak's voice came through.

"Send me the location," Rema said to her comms, then turned to Peet. "Let's go get him. We'll make sure he knows we will take him somewhere safe when we leave here. There's no need to lose him after all we've been through."

Peet nodded.

"We'll meet you all back here. If that works..."

Jarem nodded. Nelly was still appraising Zelwa.

"You all must be hungry," Zelwa finally said. "With the ship powered up, I think I can get some food prepared."

Peet's eyes lit up.

"We better get Stavo quickly if you want to eat," Rema said to Peet.

"Let's go...," Peet grinned. He'd been trying to make up for a life of missed meals ever since he and Rema joined the team.

As Peet and Rema walked away, Zelwa welcomed Jarem and Nelly into the ship.

"I guess we should head back to the mess hall," Zelwa said. Jarem couldn't help but wonder if this was some sort of trap. The ship looked pretty bare and abandoned, and he still couldn't tell if he could trust her. On the surface, she seemed like an Earther, but she also differed from them. Her eyes never darted into the night or up in the sky, as if she was afraid of what might find her.

"So, you have a ship here?" Zelwa asked. "When did you arrive?"

Nelly glared at Jarem, not wanting to share too much with Zelwa, but he shrugged. He preferred to be as honest as possible, but he would hold back some things until he knew more about the situation.

"Not long," Jarem said. "You said you had a family here?"

SHEILA LEE BROWN

Zelwa stopped walking. Jarem thought she would say more, but she turned, smiled, and pointed to the room he had found her in.

"We're here. Now let's see if I can get the food processor working."

Zelwa walked over to a wall with several small metal doors and began pressing buttons. It whirred to life.

"This is good," she said. "We haven't had access to the food processors in--"

Zelwa looked confused. Jarem thought she might be having trouble with the time anomaly she spoke of earlier.

"What are we doing?" Nelly whispered to Jarem. "Does she know anything or what?"

"I don't know," Jarem said.

"Well, is she a friend or enemy...?"

"I don't know that either," Jarem said. "I can't feel anything from her."

"Is she shielding herself somehow?"

"Maybe...," Jarem watched Zelwa as she moved along the wall, pressing buttons. "It doesn't seem likely."

120

"I should probably sterilize everything before we actually make food," Zelwa said as she pressed more buttons. "We'll be ready to go when the green light comes on."

Zelwa walked over to Jarem and Nelly and sat at the nearest table. She looked from one to the other until they sat down with her. Jarem saw her press her hand into the top of the table as if to assure herself it was really there.

"So, are you leaving soon?"

The way Zelwa asked made Jarem feel like that was exactly what she wanted. Even without feeling anything, he knew she was hiding something.

"You are welcome to come with us. I am assuming you don't want to stay here *alone*," Jarem said.

Zelwa gave him the smile again.

"I'll be fine. I have the ship, access to food and water."

"But how long will that last?" Nelly asked. "And why are you here by yourself?" Nelly leaned forward as if she were going to interrogate Zelwa.

Zelwa didn't speak, and her smile faltered.

"It's okay," Jarem said. "We really mean no harm. We're here to solve a problem." He sighed at Nelly's glare and decided to be as direct as possible. "Can you tell us what you know about the resurrects?"

"Resurrects?" Zelwa frowned.

"Maybe you call them something else," Jarem said. "I'm talking about the undead things that search out and take over all Earthers it finds."

Zelwa's eyes widened.

"Do you know something?" Nelly leaned across the table further.

"No," Zelwa said. Jarem couldn't tell if she was lying or not. She looked around the mess hall and Jarem realized she was assessing the situation. He could see the concern on her face, but not feel it. He thought he understood. She expected there to be people here, her family. And there was no one. "You think these resurrects are here? Did they...?" Zelwa jumped as the wall made a beep and the green light came on. "Do you know where my family is?"

"I do not," Jarem said. He was still hesitant to tell her there was no life on this planet when they arrived. She already looked upset. "We haven't seen anyone here other than you."

Zelwa sank back into her chair.

"We came here because we believe there is something here that will stop the resurrects," Jarem said. "Since you are the only lifeform we've encountered, we thought maybe you would know something."

Zelwa shook her head no.

"I've never heard of resurrects before," she said. "What did you mean they take over...Earthers?"

Jarem and Nelly looked at one another. Jarem wondered where Zelwa had been before she came out of the stone arch. If she really had never heard of the resurrects, maybe they could all go through the stone arch and start a new life there. One thing at a time.

"We don't know exactly what happens, but we know a couple of things. Resurrects were all once Earthers. They do not interfere with any other species, no matter how similar. Once a resurrect identifies an Earther, if it gets into close enough proximity with them, then something happens to the Earthers. They somehow pull apart the bodies and then pull them back together. Then they are a resurrect, too."

"That sounds horrible," Zelwa said. "Is it curable? Can they be healed?"

"No," Nelly said. "There is nothing left of the person in the mutilated body."

Zelwa shivered. At that moment, Peet, Rema, and Stavo walked in.

"Decided to stay around?" Nelly asked Stavo, though she was still watching Zelwa.

"I heard there was food," Stavo said. "And a ride to somewhere of my choosing."

Nelly looked at Rema and Peet and they shrugged.

"Oh, yeah, the food," Zelwa said, hopping up and walking back over to the wall. "What would you like? This food processor was coded with the most popular meals on Earth at the time we left."

Jarem and his crews looked at each other in stunned silence at the words "at the time we left." Jarem considered that the ship's data was right and that somehow she had missed the last three hundred years.

"You're welcome to pick whatever you want off the menu," Zelwa said. She turned when no one responded.

Jarem walked over and examined the many choices on the meal list. Many he had never heard of before, except in books or in databanks. He looked over at Zelwa, who was smiling again, oblivious to the shock everyone was experiencing. He tried once again to see what she was feeling and came up with nothing, so he finally asked what he knew was on everyone's mind.

"You've been to Earth?"

CHAPTER 10: THE CAVES
ZELWA

Zelwa stepped out of the spacecraft and ducked out of sight. She was having a hard time processing everything that was happening. So many things were off and she needed answers. The group she left in the mess hall was peculiar. They seemed shocked when she told them that "of course I've been to Earth. I was born there and lived there until we came here."

But then they didn't ask anything else. She could see that they wanted to. Something was up with them. She didn't think they meant any harm, but the whole situation was odd. These new people were here, but none of the people she knew were. That she could see, anyway. The ship's log had to be wrong. There was no way that so much time had passed. She needed answers and there was only one place she could think to get them: Elder.

Zelwa glanced behind her to make sure no one was following. She had set the food processors to print several of her favorite meals for them to try. She left them with plates full of spaghetti and meatballs, pizza, cheesesteak, mashed potatoes, and ice cream. Thankfully, the nutrient materials were still viable and could be processed into food forms. It bothered her that these strange people didn't seem to believe that she had been on Earth. Where had they come from? And why hadn't she ever heard of these resurrects?

While they were fixated and enthralled with the food, she had slipped away. She found the familiar path that would lead down to the caves. If the time lapse on the ship's log was right, then everyone she knew was gone. Also, she felt weird, different. She couldn't quite put her finger on what it was, but she was on edge and unsure of everything. Her memories still felt scattered from whatever she had experienced when she fell backwards. Surely that is all that had happened. The in-between time was a blur. She pressed her hand into a boulder for stability as she passed it. She could feel the hardness of the rock and how it was cooling as the evening sky darkened. It seemed pretty real.

She needed to find Elder and ask what happened. She also knew that she couldn't bring people she didn't know with her. Elder wouldn't like that. And she wasn't completely sure she should trust them.

Laris had enough light reflecting off its three moons that even with the day darkening, Zelwa easily found the trail that led to the caves. If three hundred years had passed, not much had changed. She walked up the hill. It seemed like she had just come down it, running with Mora and then having that awkward conversation with her mom. If the ship's time log was correct...what would she do? Zelwa increased her pace, rounding the curve at the top of the hill and making her way down to the entrance to the caves.

As she approached the large group of rocks where the cave opening was, she noticed it was closed off. To anyone who came to this planet, it wouldn't look like there was anything there—just a small rocky hill. Zelwa knew better. She walked up and touched the area where she remembered the door was located. An opening appeared, much taller than Zelwa. She looked up and saw Elder looking down on her. He smiled and took a step towards her.

"You are back," Elder bent down and patted Zelwa on the head. Hearing a familiar voice was soothing.

"Elder…,"

Before Zelwa could finish speaking, Elder looked out behind her and spoke sternly.

"Come out. Take care how you approach."

Zelwa turned to see Jarem and Nelly stepping out of the shadows. They had their hands and arms splayed out as if to show they were harmless. Zelwa realized she wasn't as stealthy as she thought.

"Forgive us," Jarem said. "We did not mean to lurk. I am here--"

"It does not matter to me why you are here," Elder said. "You were not invited, nor are you welcome."

"But…," Nelly began.

"You should return to your ship and leave. All of you."

"No," Jarem said, taking a firm step forward. "Too much is at stake. We came here to save our species.

Something here is meant to help us. We're not leaving until- "

"That is none of my concern," Elder said.

Jarem took another step forward and Elder raised an eyebrow slightly.

"Please," he said, and stared at Elder with awkward concentration.

Elder stared back, then spoke.

"Zelwa, please enter."

Zelwa walked into the cave and waited.

"You should leave," Elder said, then turned and stepped into the cave. "There is nothing here for *you*." And, with that, the stone around the opening merged back together as if it was never there. Zelwa felt a little bad for Jarem and his friends. However, at the moment, she needed to find her own answers.

Inside the cave, light came from above as if the cave ceiling gave off some phosphorescent glow. Zelwa wondered if she should have asked Elder to help Jarem and his friends. Elder looked down at Zelwa.

"I am glad that you are safe," he said. "I have been concerned for you."

"Thank you, Elder," Zelwa said, all thoughts about Jarem replaced with more pressing questions. "Can you please tell me what happened? Why is the ship empty already? Where are my parents? Are they okay?"

Elder frowned. He placed a large finger in the middle of Zelwa's forehead and nodded slowly.

"I see," he said. "You're still scattered. I have something to show you."

"Mora took a stone. I should have told you," Zelwa said. "Where is-?"

Zelwa didn't finish. Elder's words had an ominous quality to them. She suddenly hoped to prolong the not knowing for as long as possible.

Elder turned and began walking deeper into the cave. Zelwa followed, knowing Elder would only speak when he was ready. They continued walking. It was a path Zelwa knew well. Soon they entered the Impressing training room. Zelwa gasped at the number of stones that were now on the shelves, some in small piles. There hardly seemed room for more. In the center of the room was a larger rock as wide as Zelwa was tall, polished to a smooth shine.

"How were so many Impressings made?" Zelwa asked, walking over to the shelf Elder had once placed her stones on.

"This room isn't used anymore," Elder said. "The Impressings here were for practice. This stone contains a history." Elder pointed to the large rock in the center of the room.

Zelwa wanted to ask why the room wasn't used anymore, but she was afraid he would tell her and that the reason was because everyone was gone.

"I think it is better if you see what has happened."

Zelwa nodded, her voice muted by fear. Elder invited her to approach the large stone.

"Do you remember how to read the Impress?"

Like it was only this morning, Zelwa thought, *because it was to me, but I guess it wasn't for everyone else.* She nodded she did and walked over to the stone that was the size of a table, but yet wasn't flat...

"You may begin whenever you are ready. I will help to guide you."

Zelwa hesitated, afraid of what the truth might be. Her hand stopped an inch short of touching the stone, and she breathed deeply a few times. Did she really want to know? She gulped. Even if she didn't know, it wouldn't change the fact that she was alone now. Maybe if she knew, there was something she could do about it.

She touched the stone and slowed her breathing. She sought the energy of the stone and when she finally found it, she focused on the last day she remembered and sought what came after. It took several long minutes, but images popped into her mind and then a memory began playing. Tapping into the energy felt easier than it ever had before.

> *Zelwa was looking through the eyes of her father. She recognized his wedding ring with the funny markings on them—a language he and her mother had made up when they were young and just exploring how much they loved learning and studying other cultures. He was one of the last people on the ship for the evening. Three others were outside the loading dock, putting away the moving carts for the day and preparing to go back to the cave.*

Her father was about to switch the power saver on when a blast shook the ship and all the power turned off. He heard screams outside. He rounded a corner to see Mora floating, her back to him. The people in front of her were in pieces, legs and arms ripped away. Slowly, the pieces began to move and come back together.

Zelwa's father remained frozen. Zelwa could feel his fear and terror in the memory. Without noticing him, Mora and the reconfigured men hovered above the ground, floating in a circle. After a while, they looked upward to the sky. As one, they moved up and up. Zelwa's dad slowly emerged from the ship, trying to see where they went. Surely they couldn't have left the atmosphere without a ship. He hurried on to the caves to alert Elder and the others.

Zelwa drifted out of her father's memory but felt herself sliding into another.

"Dr. Wissinger?"

Zelwa was seeing through the eyes of her mother. She was organizing things in the rooms Elder had formed for them in the caves. Dr.

Wissinger turned to see one of the crew members.

"What is it?"

"It's your husband. He says something has happened at the ship."

Zelwa felt a pang of anxiousness in her mother's memory, but her voice was steady.

"Take me to him."

They came to her dad, talking to several other crew members.

"It was Selph, Jim, and Raldo. We've notified their partners, but we need to keep everyone inside until we know more about what is going on. They couldn't have gone far without a ship and they may harm others."

That was Zelwa's dad.

Inside her mom's memory, Zelwa felt something. The other crew members were making suggestions about what to do next, but Zelwa, caught in her mother's memories, couldn't focus on their words. Her mother's hand tightened into a fist that she placed in her *pocket to hide. When she swallowed, her throat had gone dry. Zelwa could feel an immediate uptick in her mother's heartbeat. Then her mother managed to quietly say, "Where's Zelwa?"*

Zelwa's dad looked over at his wife.

"Annette...," he began.

Zelwa's mom took a step forward.

"Where is our daughter?"

Zelwa could see her dad was breathing more heavily now. The tenseness in her mother's body felt like she was about to leap forward and attack, but she somehow still stood steady.

"We don't know," her dad said and looked down for a moment before meeting her eyes. "But I didn't see her. She wasn't there when Mora killed those men."

"We'll make a plan, a safe one, to search for her," one of the other crew said. Her mom wasn't listening. She was looking off down the tunnel. Zelwa didn't know how to process it, but it felt like something broke within her mother.

Everything around her lost focus and then the memory was mostly heart pounding and heavy breathing. When Zelwa could receive images again, she was outside the caves, running through the paths on the surface of Laris, screaming Zelwa's name over and over.

Someone suddenly pulled her backwards. She turned. It was Zelwa's dad.

"We have to get back to the caves," he said. "We'll find her, but the risk of being out here is too great at the moment."

"No! You said we'd be safe here. There are no bodies of water. There are no animals or dangerous plants. There is nothing here! We're supposed to be safe! Where's my daughter? Where is she?" Zelwa's mom was screaming and pounding Zelwa's dad with her fists. Zelwa had never seen her mom like this or knew she felt this way. It was jolting.

"Elder will help," her dad said as calmly as he could manage. Zelwa could tell he wasn't sure, but didn't have anything else to offer. "He will locate her more quickly than us now that our

equipment isn't working. Zelwa is smart and capable. She's probably in one of her little hiding places where she goes to think."

Zelwa flinched outside the memory. She hadn't realized they knew about that.

"No-no-no-no-no-no. NOOOOOOOOOOOOOOOOOOOO!" her mother screamed and collapsed into her father's arms.

The immense pain of her mother's emotion startled Zelwa out of the memory. She needed a moment to process it, that her mother actually cared about her, but didn't have time to dwell on it before she drifted into another memory. She was seeing through her father again. He was in their rooms, sitting and waiting, when Zelwa's mother walked in.

"You went out again," he said as she hung her face scarf on a hook.

"Yes," was all she said.

"I'm worried about you," her dad said. "It's been months."

"I'm not going to give up."

"I know," her dad said. "We've lost too much. I don't want to lose each other." Her dad walked over and hugged Zelwa's mother. She stood rigid. He relaxed his grip. "Tomorrow I will go out with you." Zelwa's mom looked at her husband in surprise. "Yes. We will go out looking for her together."

The memory shifted again. Still her dad's point of view.

Her dad and mom were with the medic, Nurse Asmine. He was feeling excited. Her mother looked grim. Nurse Asmine walked out of the room for a moment.

"Everything seems okay," her dad said. "How are you feeling?"

"How can we do this?" her mom said, clutching her midsection, and what Zelwa realized was the beginnings of a pregnancy. "I can't do this again."

"We'll do it together," her dad said. "No distractions this time."

"I don't know if I can," her mom said, beginning to cry. The display of emotions sent a shockwave through Zelwa. "Maybe we were not

meant to have children. Maybe I'm not meant to have children."

Nurse Asmine walked back in. Zelwa's mom didn't bother to wipe her tears. Nurse Asmine put a hand on Zelwa's mom's shoulder.

"I know you've been through a lot, Annette."

She used Zelwa's mom's first name and didn't get a glare!

"We are here to support you in whatever you want to do. This is surely difficult." Nurse Asmine moved to sit down and face Zelwa's parents. "You take whatever time you need to process what is happening." She paused as if uncertain how to continue, then said, "I am hoping to give you a new possibility, a new perspective, and…maybe a new adventure."

"And what is that?" Zelwa's mom sounded tired, but also somewhat curious.

"If you are open and ready for it, I think there's a whole new experience available to us here."

"What do you mean?" That was Zelwa's father.

"You're not the only ones expecting a child,"
Nurse Asmine said.

"Okay," Zelwa's mom said.

Nurse Asmine smiled.

"You don't understand," she went on. "Every
male-female couple that came with the mission
is expecting a child. We're about to give birth to
a whole new generation. That's got to be more
than a coincidence."

"We're all pregnant at the same time?" Zelwa's
mom asked in amazement.

"Yes," Nurse Asmine said. "Different expected
arrival dates, but close enough to each other to
be notable."

Zelwa's mom and dad looked at one another.

"We haven't had contact with Earth in nearly a
year," Nurse Asmine went on. "We're about to
have a lot of children running around. This is a
colony now. And while we've done a lot here,
we don't have a lot of structures in place to
expand or manage all the resources we will
need."

"We have enough specialists with us to come up with something," Zelwa's dad said slowly. "It just needs some organization."

"We'll need something in place to ensure knowledge is passed down effectively," Zelwa's mom said. Zelwa could see a familiar gleam in her eye that she always had when starting a new project.

The next few memories flowed by quickly, reminding Zelwa of her experience falling through the arch.

Her mom holding a newborn and smiling.

Her mom and dad with three more children and the rest of the crew with their children celebrating some milestone in growing food and building out the caves.

The children grown up, Impressings becoming second nature.

The grown-up children having children. Population expanding. A young man's face passed into view at the end. He reminded Zelwa of her father.

Zelwa jerked herself out of the memories. She opened her eyes and turned to Elder. The emotions were fading, but the basic truth the memories told was clear.

"My parents are dead."

Elder didn't answer. He didn't have to. Zelwa still felt some residual emotions from the memories of her parents, but realized that she didn't feel much else except hollowness. Her parents were dead. Zelwa thought back to the experience of falling and drifting that she thought was a dream. Could some part of her parents have tried to reach out to her...?

"What did Mora do?"

"She was curious," Elder said. "I know that about your species. She was creative long before I expected,. Maybe she was called to do it?"

"What do you mean?"

"The rocks and stones you work with are not without their own feelings and ambitions," Elder said.

"The stones are conscious?"

"Not fully in the way you mean," Elder said. "This planet is in its fledgling state. But, yes, the stones have a growing awareness."

Zelwa thought to ask why Elder had her and the others Impress information into the stones but became distracted by the sound of distant childish laughter. She looked at Elder to see if he had heard it as well.

"That sound. Are the descendants still here?"

Elder nodded yes.

"Can I meet them?"

"Of course. They are your family."

Elder motioned for Zelwa to follow him. She did. He never asked her about where she had been or what she had experienced, which she thought was odd. Of course, maybe he already knew from when he touched her forehead earlier. She thought again about how her parents had shown up when she was drifting. Was it possible she had somehow connected to their spirits? Again, Zelwa thought she should feel more, but she felt hollow inside. Maybe she stalled out because there was so much for her to take in.

She settled into the familiarity of the hallway tunnels. They finally arrived at the opening that Zelwa remembered being much smaller and bare, with various rooms for the crew members to move into. Now it was an elaborate chamber that looked like a small city had grown up out of the rock. People and light and joyful sounds filled the paths between the various homes and porches and tunnels and stairways, moving upward and all around. This was so much more advanced than what Elder had originally built for them. Many of the stones had rich colors and glinted with metallic bits.

When Elder walked out into the open with Zelwa, the nearby people all stopped to stare with open curiosity. They seemed happy and harmless. A young man stepped forward. Zelwa was startled to see the last face she had seen in the Impressing stone. Seeing him made all she had experienced in the memories more real. The young man looked slightly older than Zelwa, with broad shoulders and his hair pulled back in a ponytail. He truly resembled Zelwa's father. Zelwa had the thought that this was how Timon might have looked like if he had gotten older. She caught herself staring and looked away, embarrassed.

Zelwa took in the rest of the people there, noticing no one was wearing a uniform. They wore loose-fitting material that looked very comfortable, similar to what Elder wore.

"Thames," Elder said. "You will be the perfect host for Zelwa. She has returned to be with her family."

Thames nodded to Elder and Elder took his leave. Thames eyed Zelwa as if he was waiting for her to say something.

"Leave it to Elder to give the most basic introduction," Zelwa said after he had disappeared around the corner, expecting her to figure out how to navigate the situation. She was uncomfortable around so many unknown people. It was stranger than Jarem's small group. Thames smiled and she relaxed a bit. She supposed she was his great-great something or other.

"This is unusual," Thames said. "You have time traveled?"

Zelwa thought Thames was accepting the situation a little too easily.

"I guess," she said. "I don't really know what happened."

"Yes, your history has been a mystery for a long time," Thames said. "I will show you around and we can talk about it."

Zelwa followed Thames as he began walking down the path nearest them. He began pointing out people and saying their names. Zelwa felt overwhelmed and didn't even try to remember them all,. She could see bits and pieces of her former crew in many of the features. What they had created was quite remarkable. The basic living areas that Elder had designed had been individualized—some were ornate, and some had a more organic look, depending, Zelwa supposed, on the tastes of the person.

"Where do you get water to grow the food?" she asked.

"The surface of the planet is quite dry, but inside the caves we have condensation that began developing and we purify it and use it."

"I don't think we knew about that when I was here before. We were worried about what water we had left."

"We've come a long way since then," Thames said with a smile. "We are self-sufficient now."

"Do you always stay in the caves?" Zelwa wasn't sure she should tell Thames about Jarem and his group. "I didn't see any sign of life on the surface of the planet except our old ship."

"Elder doesn't like us to go outside the cave. He does not think it is safe for us."

"Is he worried about the resurrects?"

"Resurrects?"

"The things Mora created...?" Zelwa said.

"Maybe," Thames said. "I'll tell you a secret. I have been to the arch. And I have wandered the surface of the planet."

"Why? What if those things came back? It sounds horrible."

"Sometimes we have to know things for ourselves," he said. "It might be dangerous. It also might be exactly what's needed for understanding. You don't know unless you try."

"That sounds stupid," Zelwa said. "Sorry. I didn't mean that to come out so rude." She looked down, thinking of Timon and Mora. "My observation of curiosity in action hasn't been exactly rewarding. Maybe there's a safer way to be curious?"

"Perhaps," he said. "I've studied our history, or at least what we know of it. It seems like those who take chances are the ones that advance us as a civilization. Sometimes the cost of that is the person's life, but we all learn from it. Someone eats the berry and dies. We know it is poison. We build things that fail until it succeeds. It takes more than passing fancy. These people pushing things forward seem to feel driven from something inside."

That made Zelwa think of Jarem and how determined he was to find answers. And now she knew them. She didn't see how it would help him, but she thought if she told him, he could leave, knowing he had achieved what he came to find out.

"I...I have to go," Zelwa said.

"Where?" Thames said. "I haven't showed you everything yet."

Zelwa hesitated, trying to think of a reason to leave.

"You are maybe planning to leave the caves? Would Elder like you to do so?" He leaned in mischievously. "What is driving you, young ancestor?"

He was smiling, but Zelwa kinda wanted to punch him in the face.

"I'm just being a decent human being," Zelwa muttered as she turned and began making her way out, not really caring if anyone noticed. Thames followed. "I was exploring this planet before you were even thought about. I don't need a guide." She wasn't sure he had heard her, but then he spoke again.

"Then you continue to take us forward, sister."

The words jolted Zelwa, and she turned back to Thames. He didn't seem to realize what he had said. *Sister.* Maybe it was because he looked a lot like her father and that she had had the thought about Timon earlier. She knew he wasn't Timon, but being called sister had a strange effect on her. And she felt a sort of sisterly annoyance with him. He bowed his head to her and walked away. Zelwa realized she was being silly. She had heard several of the cave people calling each other brother and sister as they passed by them.

She turned and began walking again, making her way to the exit. She let her fingers graze the right side of the cave. It felt real. Too real. She couldn't even pretend this wasn't happening now. She thought she should be more upset, but she just felt neutral. Directionless. What was she was going to say to Jarem? Would he be disappointed? Would he have other ideas to help his friends?

The main thing that kept coming up again and again was that she didn't fit anywhere any longer.

I'm no longer a sister. I'm no longer a daughter. Who am I? What purpose do I serve? I'm nobody. Maybe I can help Jarem and his friends, but then what?

She wasn't sure what the answer was, but at the moment, it gave her a reason to keep moving.

CHAPTER 11: DECISIONS
JAREM

Jarem and Nelly made their way back towards Zelwa's ship. Jarem sensed Peet and Rema as near the ship's entrance. They had hidden in the surrounding rocks.

"Where's Stavo?" Nelly asked.

"Inside," Rema said. "Exploring his Earther side through food."

"At the rate he's going, Zelwa's not going to have much to survive on," Peet said. "The nutrient stores aren't unlimited."

"I think Zelwa has other options," Jarem said. He couldn't hide his disappointment in the situation.

"What happened?" Rema asked.

Jarem told them about Elder and the entranceway into the planet.

"That's odd," Peet said. "Dr. Yac's scan should have picked up his lifeform, even if he was below the surface."

"I suspect a being like Elder may have ways to avoid being noticed if that is what he wants," Jarem said. "The real question is what do we do now? We came all this way. Experienced all this loss." Jarem placed a hand on Nelly's shoulder. Peet pulled Rema closer to him. Nelly nodded that she was okay. For now. "Something is here for us. I know it. I just don't know how we're going to find it."

"You really couldn't get anything from him?" Nelly asked.

Jarem shook his head. He had attempted, feebly, to communicate telepathically with the being Zelwa called Elder. It was like hitting an impenetrable fortress. He was no match for this being. Jarem was actually beginning to think all his training may have been pointless. He had only been successful in defending against a low-level being like Sloctum.

After the opening into the planet closed, Jarem walked over and felt the rock where the door had been. If he hadn't seen it, he wouldn't have known it had been there.

"Not everything we do is successful," Nelly finally said, turning and letting Jarem's hand fall from her shoulder. "We could go back and figure out what to do next."

"Not everything we do has so much riding on it," Jarem responded.

"Zelwa may have been our best lead, but we've lost her," Nelly said. "What about the people on Hanu? The resurrects could have found them."

"They are well hidden. Resurrects have come through before and not found them," Peet said.

"But resurrects like Kin? What if it knows what Kin knows?" She turned away from everyone as her words sent a shiver through the team.

"If that's the case," Rema spoke in a small voice. "We would be all that is left. It would be best if we didn't go back."

The words hung in the air as they all contemplated the possibility.

"Maybe if we all went back to the place where the opening was. We could meditate or focus our energy," Rema said.

"For what? For him to come out and tell us to leave again?" Nelly kicked at a boulder angrily.

"With Tock and Kin lost," Rema said softly, "we owe it to their memory and what they gave up to try with whatever we have to work with. Right now, all we have is our determination."

"Rema's right," Peet said. "We don't know what is happening on Hanu right now. And I know we don't know what we're looking for here. But we are here and if something is to change, this is it. We can't give that up easily."

"What do you think?" Jarem asked Nelly. She was still turned away. She kicked the boulder again, but then let out a ragged breath and seemed to shake something off.

"Fine," she said, turning to look at Jarem. "How do you want to do this?"

Back to being the leader, Jarem thought. He missed Tock more than ever.

"Rema's idea could work," Jarem said. "And she's right. It's really all we have to work with." Jarem looked to Peet. "Unless you have any tech-assisted ideas."

Peet shook his head.

"I don't think forcing our way into the planet is going to get us the results we want. And I feel like we would be going in blind anyway, since our readings may not be accurate of what is under the surface."

"I agree. Forcing will not work," Jarem said. "We could go back and peacefully meditate on our purpose outside the area where the opening appeared."

"Maybe this Elder will either change his mind or at least be annoyed enough to come out and talk to us," Rema said.

"Or just get rid of us," Nelly said. She looked at Jarem. "What he said sounded like a threat to me."

"I'm not sure," Jarem said. "Perhaps it was. I don't have any better ideas and this feels like it could work. A group meditation might do us all some good."

"What about Stavo?" Rema asked. "I don't know that we should leave him here alone."

"Do you think he'll want to join us?" Jarem asked.

"We should at least check with him," Rema said.

"I'll get him," Peet said and went inside the ship to find Stavo.

"We're really close to something," Jarem said. "I can feel it."

"Me, too," Rema said.

They looked at Nelly and she nodded in the affirmative.

We're going to be a bit longer, Jarem sent to Dr. Yac. He was sure that Peet was keeping Dr. Yac updated, but it didn't hurt to let him know. Jarem sent telepathic images of their plan.

Be cautious, Dr. Yac responded. *I am concerned about this being that is unreadable. I am also curious about the arch you found and the Earther that came from it. I will perform my own assessment.*

"Dr. Yac is going to observe the arch and see if he notices anything we missed," Jarem said.

"Good," Nelly said.

"We'll have multiple possibilities covered," Rema said. "We will crack this puzzle."

"I like that attitude," Peet said, walking out of the ship with Stavo. "He's coming with us."

"This isn't the sort of planet I would want to be alone on," Stavo said as he followed Peet and joined the group. "It feels dead."

The five began walking back towards the caves. With a full belly, Stavo seemed to be more talkative.

"I don't know that I'll be much use to you meditating," Stavo said. "But I can stand watch. I don't expect much to happen, but I can keep an eye out."

"Thanks, Stavo," Rema said.

"You know," Stavo went on. "Maybe you all are going about this all wrong. Resurrects have no interest in me because of my mixed genetics. Perhaps diluting the DNA of pure Earthers with other species would stop them. The future generations would be safe."

"Interesting idea," Peet said.

"And what if they adapt?" Nelly asked.

"And how are we supposed to convince other species to cooperate with that kind of risk?" Rema added. "Why should we be deciding about who we want a family with based on their genetics?"

"It was only an idea," Stavo said. "If you'd seen as many Earthers taken as I have…"

"We've seen our share," Nelly said softly. That wasn't quite true. Sure, they had all lost people—lots of them. They all hadn't really seen it happen up close like Stavo had. They just knew that it had when they glimpsed a familiar resurrect or if someone never made it back to a safe spot.

The walk back to the caves became more quiet, just the sound of footsteps. Jarem thought of his own encounter with the resurrects as a child, before the Yacca. He knew many people who had been taken, but he had seen it happen up close. Just the one time, but it was enough.

It didn't take them long to make it back to the caves. They sat facing each other in a sort of square position. Stavo stood to the side, watching it all.

"Everybody ready to begin?" Jarem asked. He could feel nervousness and doubt, but at the bottom of all, there was hope. That is what they would work with. Jarem smiled. "We're not done yet."

"And we will keep going," Nelly said with determination. Rema and Peet nodded in agreement.

The four Earthers controlled their breathing, syncing their inhales and exhales.

"Focus on the goal," Jarem whispered when he felt the shift into relaxation from the group. "Focus on the future we wish to create. See it as a possibility. See it as real. The opportunity is showing up for us as expected."

The group breathed in and out. Jarem felt himself drift in his imagining of the life he wanted to experience with his fellow Earthers. Blue skies, trees, plants of Earth. The ocean. An entire planet that provided everything they needed to live, thrive, and grow. It felt like the meditation went on and on.

"Something's happening," Stavo whispered as he nudged Jarem.

Jarem opened his eyes and turned to see what Stavo was looking at. Nelly was already on her feet. The door to the cave had opened.

Zelwa stepped out.

CHAPTER 12: ANOTHER UNWELCOME SURPRISE

ZELWA

"You came back. I didn't think you would," Jarem said as he stood to face Zelwa. Rema and Peet were up as well.

"I'm sorry," Zelwa said as she stepped out and the opening closed behind her. "I know Elder was a little off-putting. He doesn't like to be surprised. And this is his planet. He only allows what he wants to allow."

"His planet?"

"Yes. He is cultivating it."

"Doesn't look like he's doing much," Peet said.

"I know it seems that way. When my parents came here, Elder offered an opportunity to study with him. He can Impress information into stones and minerals and cause them to hold data or shift to his will." Zelwa frowned and looked back at the rock wall behind her. "He probably wouldn't want me telling you that."

"We've all seen how the cave opening happened," Jarem said. "But why are you out here?"

Zelwa took a moment to look them over. The one Jarem called Nelly was super tense. Rema and Peet stood near each other. They seemed curious. The other guy was just standing around. They didn't seem like bad people. And she was right about him not giving up. She hadn't been completely surprised to see them when she opened the wall. She nodded to herself. This was the right decision.

"I think I know what you came here to find out. I just don't know that it will help you much."

"You learned something about the resurrects? Is there a way to stop them?" That was Nelly.

Zelwa shook her head.

"I don't know what can be done about them. But I can tell you one thing about them." Zelwa paused, suddenly worried about all the questions that might come from her next statement. Some of those she wouldn't be able to answer and maybe wouldn't want to answer. She looked at their expectant faces and realized she had to give them something. She had committed to it. "It all started here."

"How?" Jarem said after a heavy pause.

Zelwa didn't answer. She wasn't sure how much she should tell these strangers. And she didn't want to give anything away about the people still on the planet.

"I don't know much," she finally said. "Only that it began here with a friend of mine. Mora did something with the stones that she wasn't supposed to do. I don't know how it happened. I fell backwards and when I landed, I was still in the same place, but she was gone and a lot of time has passed. "

Jarem was silent.

"Does that mean your family...?"

Zelwa gulped, but didn't speak. She didn't want to lie, but she couldn't tell them everything.

"My family is dead."

"I'm sorry," Jarem said.

He's looking at me weird again. They probably think it was the resurrects, Zelwa thought.

"So how do you know the resurrects started here?" Rema asked.

Zelwa swallowed again. The air seemed drier than ever.

"Did Elder tell you?" Nelly asked.

Zelwa nodded. That was mostly true.

"Whatever Mora did...she became...a resurrect...and left the planet with others. I guess that is when they began hunting down other...Earthers."

Jarem turned to look at his team. Before he could speak, Zelwa continued.

"Whatever happened, happened at the stone arch," she said. "The arch wasn't there until...until Mora did what she did."

Jarem turned back to Zelwa.

"Do you remember anything about the time you weren't here? We saw you come out of that arch."

"It felt like a...dream," Zelwa said. That seemed safe enough to tell him. And she wanted to tell somebody. The memory was haunting her.

"Do you think it might be something we could all go through?" Rema asked. "Maybe we could come back at a time where the resurrects are no longer a threat."

"I don't know," Zelwa said. "I don't know how Mora did what she did. Maybe Elder does, but he won't help with that. He won't interfere."

"Sounds like some Yacca I know," Peet said with a sad smile.

Jarem put his face in his hands and then ran them up and through his hair.

"I don't know what to do," he said to the team. "Maybe we should investigate the stone arch again. Perhaps we missed something. Dr. Yac is there now."

"That is where Mora was the last time I saw her." Zelwa picked up a palm-sized rock lying on the ground near her feet. "To think all our lives were disrupted by something as small as this." She looked at it, flipping it over in her hand once or twice. She felt a familiar tingle just below the surface. "This place feels wilder than it did before. I think this is ready for Impressing."

Zelwa looked up, embarrassed, feeling she had said too much.

"What is Impressing?" Jarem asked.

Zelwa took a step backwards towards the caves. She touched the stone and the opening appeared.

"I've probably said more than I should. I just wanted to tell you what I learned about the resurrects. Maybe it will help you. I hope so, but I am going to go back to the caves now. If you try to come in without Elder's permission...let's just say, you won't like it."

"We won't try to come in," Jarem said. He turned to look at his team. Nelly didn't look like she was in complete agreement, but she nodded. Jarem took a step towards Zelwa, his hands up to reassure her. "First, thank you for coming out to tell us what you discovered. I don't want to push you, but would you consider staying with us and help us figure it out? If you go back inside, we don't have a way to contact you. And right now you're the only link we have to what happened."

Zelwa considered it. Everything in the cave would be there for her later, no matter how long she took with Jarem and his team. And it felt kind of good to be needed. Maybe she had a purpose to serve after all. For a little while.

"What will you do if you can stop the resurrects? What then?" she asked.

"When it's done, we get to figure it out," Jarem said.

"We can find other Earthers that have been running away. Let them know they are safe from resurrects. Give them a chance at a home," Rema said.

"We could go back to Earth if we wanted," Peet said. "Explore it. We could stay where we are. Or travel. We can choose."

"We can stop running," Nelly said. "And rest."

Zelwa nodded. They were all admirable goals. She wasn't sure what she could do to help with it.

"Dr. Yac will wait for us at the arch," Peet said, tapping his wristband. "Now that we have a lead, we should start heading that way."

"Go on ahead," Jarem said. "I would like a few minutes alone with Zelwa."

Rema, Stavo, and Peet began walking away. Nelly hung back for a moment, but then followed the group.

Zelwa felt a little uncomfortable being alone with Jarem. She still had the open cave at her back if she wanted to step in and just become another person inside the planet. Something held her there. Maybe she fit in more with this group of people that didn't have any attachment to anything that was left in this world.

"Is everyone on Earth really gone?" Zelwa asked. It seemed safer to ask Jarem alone than with the group.

"Yes," Jarem said.

The idea didn't seem possible. When Zelwa had left, it had been a bustling world, full of billions of people.

"We're told that's the first place the resurrects appeared—almost as if they were drawn there."

"All those people..." Zelwa frowned. "I had friends there and other family. It's strange to think they are all gone. If the mission here had gone well, we probably would have gone back to share what we learned from Elder."

"If we go back to Earth, and I'm sure many will want to do that—to have a planet of our own again–there will be a lot of work to do. We'll have to rebuild, reestablish societies," Jarem said.

"This is really overwhelming," Zelwa said. "I'm really sorry you all have had to live the way you did. I wish it never happened. The thought that it started here… I don't know what to say. Nothing can make it better."

Zelwa thought of her brother and the devastation that came with his individual death. Jarem was talking about the death of most Earth humans.

 "Regardless of how it started," Jarem said, "we know we want it to change, that we want to take control of destiny. We know there is something here and, because of you, we have a direction to look in. We grieve for the past, but we long for a future of our choosing."

"I feel like I should feel more," Zelwa said. "I think something is wrong with me." She looked up to see Jarem watching her closely, but he didn't say anything for a while.

"Will you come with us?" he finally asked.

Zelwa was about to answer when she noticed something floating down from the atmosphere. It was a small spacecraft with what looked like a group of humanoid shapes encased in some sort of force field hovering beside it. Jarem turned to see what had caught her attention and his eyes widened to full capacity. It was coming right for them.

"Resurrects!" He began pushing Zelwa into the caves. "How do we close it?"

Zelwa could feel something tugging at her as the beings came close enough to move towards the cave entrance. She felt hypnotized by their movement towards them.

"Please Zelwa," Jarem said, tugging on her arm. "If we don't close them out now, they will attack. After everything I've told you, are you ready for that?"

That brought Zelwa back to reality. She began running with Jarem behind her. She touched the wall of the cave walls and they ran and glanced to make sure the opening was closing and noticed that several of the creatures had already made it in.

"Faster," Jarem said. They were running toward the Impressing room. If they got there fast enough, they could close themselves off. But then Zelwa considered the others in the caves that Jarem didn't know about. Would Elder protect them if the resurrects found them?

They ran faster, but Zelwa could feel the tugging as if her energy was being drained. It increased as the resurrects got closer. Something about it was familiar to her, and she suddenly wasn't as afraid as she felt she should be from the stories she had heard. She could see she and Jarem were nearing the Impressing room off to the side. She pushed him in and closed the door before he could say or do anything.

Zelwa turned to face the resurrects. There were two of them, floating above the floor of the cave, their glaring red eyes unnatural, their clothes blood soaked where the shoulders and legs had once been severed and then reconnected. She felt the tugging again. Stronger than before. Up close, they looked like something out of a nightmare. Where the eyes should have been white, they were blood-red and had a strange glow. They moved closer, and Zelwa was now truly terrified. They were so close to her and so was that tugging feeling. She closed her eyes tight and put up her hands to protect herself.

CHAPTER 13: FREAK OUT
JAREM

Jarem stumbled into a room with shelves of stones and a large stone table in the middle of the room. He spun to see the opening closing and that Zelwa was not inside. He ran over to beat on the wall as he called for her.

He felt helpless, not knowing how to get out and knowing what was about to happen to her on the other side. He placed his hand on the wall and tried to will it open. Nothing happened. He tried to reach out to Dr. Yak to warn his friends. Nothing.

"Zelwa!" he yelled, not thinking about the fact that he was giving his location away to the resurrects. How long would they wait outside for him? He thought about how he had prepared to fight them. If that door opened and they were out there, he would need to be ready.

He felt panic working its way through his body. How had they found them so quickly? And why was there a spaceship?

The closeness of the resurrects had his adrenaline racing uncontrollably and yet he was safe. Unlike Zelwa. He had the thought that maybe she had kept running, that she knew of another place to hide. Not knowing what was going on was almost worse than knowing. The situation brought up a memory when he was in a similar scenario. That situation had led him into Sloctum's clutches and onto the selling block. It had also put him in a place where he could connect with the Yacca. He tried to focus on the moment and what he should do next, but his mother's face kept popping back into his mind.

She had found a cubby in the wall just big enough for him. She hid him there, knowing there was nowhere for her to go and knowing that the resurrects would surely find her. What she didn't know was that he could see through a crack all that happened after she had hidden him. He saw the resurrect drift into the room. She had hunched down in a corner, but there was nowhere to run or shield herself. She glanced at the cubby, mouthing the words "I love you, I love you" over and over. It almost seemed to Jarem that their eyes met just before her limbs exploded from her body and then were pulled back to the torso. What was once his mother rose and joined the other resurrect as they left the room to search for more Earthers. Only years of survival had kept Jarem immobile. He had stayed in that cubby for hours before attempting to venture out, his legs cramped and his stomach growling. Sloctum had found him scrounging for food in a trash pile.

Jarem beat at the rock wall of the cave. They were so close to figuring this out. And the closer they got, the more the resurrects were showing up. It made him angry. The anger helped him focus. He stood in front of the door, placing his hands where he knew the opening had been. He slowed his breathing. He wasn't able to help his mother, but maybe it wasn't too late to help Zelwa if he could figure out how to get the door open. Jarem tried to feel for anything that might help him. He tried and tried, straining against the rock, feeling for the slightest anomaly that might help him. He stopped for a moment, unsure what else to do. Jarem turned to the rocks in the room and wondered if there was something for him there. Then he heard something outside the wall. A thump. A thump would be unusual for a resurrect that never seemed to come into physical contact with anything.

As he was about to try the door again, placing his hands on it and leaning into the rock, it came open and he lost his balance and almost fell through.

Zelwa was sitting on the floor by the door, sobbing. The two resurrects lay in a pile in front of her, motionless.

"Zelwa, are you okay?" He moved to help her if needed. She brushed him away.

"I'm fine," she said.

Jarem looked at the resurrects. He had never seen or heard of anything like this. As far as he knew, there were billions upon billions of resurrects floating through the cosmos.   .

"What happened?"

"I—I don't know," Zelwa said, wiping her eyes and attempting to stand.

Jarem helped her up, but was acutely aware of two things. One, he could feel some small emotion from her now and it was a mix of guilt, fear, and shame.

He could also tell she was lying.

CHAPTER 14: A CONNECTION
ZELWA

Zelwa allowed Jarem to help her into the Impressing Room. She closed the door behind them even though she wasn't particularly worried about the resurrects any longer.

Jarem was watching her closely, and it made her uncomfortable. She was sure he knew she was hiding something, but she wasn't ready to tell him what had happened. She needed time to process it for herself.

"Are you sure you're okay?" Jarem asked.

Zelwa nodded.

"I just need a minute," she said.

Jarem gave her some space, taking a moment to look at all the stones in the room. Zelwa could almost feel the deluge of questions he wanted to ask. His watchfulness had an excitement to it.

"Can you tell me more about the resurrects?" Zelwa asked. "Are there as many of them as there were people on Earth?"

"We think so," Jarem said, turning to Zelwa. "They can be found throughout galaxies. No bodies have ever been found discarded." Jarem paused. "Until today. Out there." He pointed to the wall where the door had closed behind them.

"No one has stopped them?" Zelwa asked.

Jarem watched Zelwa for a moment. She found she couldn't look him in the eyes.

"Today is the first time I've ever heard of them being stopped."

Zelwa sighed and looked down at her shoes.

"There are so many evolved beings. I can't believe no one has stopped them before?"

"The ones that would haven't been able to. Resurrects seem to move in short bursts outside of space and time to avoid weaponry. The more advanced beings won't help because of cosmic law. They think it is up to Earthers to save themselves. Others try to profit from it or use us as a source of amusement."

No one else could stop them, Zelwa thought. *But I did.*

The thought was overwhelming. And not because she felt the pressure of being someone who could stop them all, but because she now knew something horrifying about the resurrects.

It was her fault. She didn't know how, but it was.

Images of her brother came floating back into her mind, the loss of her parents, but also the happiness they experienced after she was gone. Why was her life so full of death? What was wrong with her?

Zelwa felt some emotion bubbling up. Grief. Anger. It wasn't as intense as she thought it would be, but it made her realize she hadn't been feeling very much since she fell through the arch. It was quite a jolt.

Zelwa hugged herself, backing to the wall and slipping down to the floor. Jarem was quickly beside her. He offered his shoulder and she leaned into it. It was nice to feel like someone cared. And weird that it came from a complete stranger.

"You should probably stay away from me," Zelwa said through tears flowing down her cheeks. "People around me get hurt."

Jarem was quiet for several moments.

"None of us that are left are strangers to hurt," he said softly. "Or fear." He moved so he was in front of Zelwa and could look her in the eyes.

"I apologize. I cannot help you ease your pain at the moment," he said. "With the resurrects on the planet, my friends are in danger and I need to get to them or get a message to them. It may already be too late. Can you tell me what happened out there?" He nodded toward the door.

Zelwa didn't speak. She turned her head to avoid his gaze. What would he think of her if he knew?

"It's okay," Jarem said. His face contorted in an inner struggle. Zelwa couldn't tell if he was upset with her or just...afraid?

"Maybe those were the only two that got through," Zelwa finally said, wiping the tears from her face.

"There's another exit for the caves. It won't come out as close to the ship as the one we came in, but we should be able to get around and maybe avoid the resurrects."

Jarem nodded slowly.

"We have to do something," he finally said. "Would Elder help us?"

Zelwa shook her head no. Hopefully, he had sealed off the rest of the colony to keep them safe. But based on her experience with him, he definitely wouldn't get involved.

"Higher beings…"

Zelwa pushed herself up and tried some quick deep breathing to calm herself. Feeling more clearheaded, she opened the door back to the tunnel and she and Jarem peeked out.

The tunnel was empty except for the bodies of the resurrects. Zelwa attempted to quell her nausea as they passed by slowly and made their way to the next turn. The legs and arms had fallen loosely to the sides of the body, no longer held together by whatever had held them together. Zelwa was glad to be out of sight of the bodies as they continued.

She almost hoped they would run into Elder so she could ask questions or get his help. But she was also sure that Elder would conveniently not be around for this.

Jarem was silent as they walked slowly, looking back and forward for any movement. As they turned the next corner, Zelwa was stunned to see three resurrects ahead. They turned as one and began moving towards them.

Zelwa felt Jarem's hand on her arm, trying to pull her back and away. She felt it slipping away as, instead, she moved towards the resurrects.

Time seemed to move more slowly, and she felt like she was moving in the dream again. The resurrects were nearly upon her. She could feel them and the energy running through them and around them. It wanted to come to her.

She wasn't afraid this time, and she took some moments to really look at them, how the energy that surrounded them protected them and created a medium in which they could float and be preserved.

After hearing them described, it was strange to see them this close up. The surrounding energy had a glow to it. Zelwa wondered if anyone else saw it the same way she did. She took a moment to notice how the strands of their hair floated within the energy like they were in water. The arms and legs, loose in their sockets, floated in a similar way. They were like puppets manipulated by energy. *That must be what protects them,* Zelwa thought. Other than the torn limbs and red eyes, it didn't appear as if the bodies had decomposed any further than the moment of their demise.

Enough observation, Zelwa thought. *Time to do something about this.*

With Zelwa's next inhale, she tugged at the energy in a way that she didn't understand, but that felt natural. It flowed from the resurrects and surged into her. The resurrects stopped, their red eyes emotionless and undead, then they abruptly collapsed, coming apart as the energy that held them together finished moving into Zelwa.

Zelwa leaned against the closest wall, another wave of grief hitting her. She couldn't hold back her sobbing. After a moment, she turned to Jarem, expecting to see hatred and fear in his eyes. Surely he must realize what had happened. That everything somehow stemmed from her. Instead, she saw hope.

CHAPTER 15: THE FIGHT
JAREM

Seeing the resurrects drop was life changing and Jarem could see possibility in their future.

"You did that," he said when he found his voice again.

Zelwa didn't respond. She was crying again. He was on the verge of asking her if she was okay when he felt it again. There was emotion for him to read and it was stronger this time. He was surprised to feel more guilt and shame. Why would she feel guilty for stopping something that was going to kill them?

It was something he and his friends had thought about for a long time and could never figure out. Zelwa had somehow dissolved the force field protecting the resurrects. Without that, they seemed to come a part. The Yacca has told them that the energy around the resurrects felt feral. It was not rational and only sought to survive. In the end, it was them against the Earthers. One would win out. Jarem was now more hopeful that it could be the Earthers.

Jarem moved closer to Zelwa and attempted to comfort her. She shook him off and he stepped away to give her space.

"I just want to make sure you're okay," Jarem said. He looked down at the fallen resurrects and felt a surge of hope again. Zelwa was at the coordinates they were sent to. She must be what would stop the resurrects. Jarem thought he might cry, too, but from happiness.

Jarem turned back to Zelwa. She was no longer leaning on the cave wall. Jarem wondered if now that he could feel her, if he could also help her in the way he helped his team.

"I'm sorry," Zelwa said. She was standing still and not looking at Jarem.

"Why are you sorry?" Jarem asked. "You saved us."
You could save us all, he thought, but didn't want to

say it out loud just yet. He could still feel her emotions were raw, and he didn't want to send any energy her way just yet.

"No," she said, still not looking at him. "I'm sorry for it all. It's my fault. All of it."

"I don't understand?" Jarem asked.

"It's me," she said quietly.

"What do you mean?"

"The resurrects," Zelwa said. She finally looked up at Jarem. "I think they are me."

He felt so much certainty from her that he stepped back in surprise. But there was also no feeling of danger from her.

"Why would you think that?" Jarem asked. "You only just appeared."

Zelwa was silent for several moments, but then spoke.

"When I first encountered the resurrects, I felt something from them. Energy? I don't know the word to use. It is sort of like when I'm Impressing a stone. Afterwards, I can still feel myself in the stone—just a little, but I know which stone is my stone and my memories."

Jarem sat down near Zelwa and tapped into her emotions. He felt her fear. He considered how she must feel, thinking that she was connected to the resurrects somehow.

"I don't really know or understand what is happening," Jarem said, "but I know you and the resurrects are not the same."

"I think some part of us is the same," Zelwa said.

"You felt yourself in the resurrects? Could you feel what they were feeling?" Jarem asked.

Zelwa shook her head no.

"But I could feel an energy there that was me and it wanted to come back," Zelwa said. "I don't know how to describe it, but I tugged at it just a little and it all came flooding back to me, leaving the resurrects with nothing to hold them together."

"It's strange," Jarem said carefully. "But it is also kind of wonderful."

"There's nothing wonderful about discovering that some part of you caused the destruction of humanity."

Jarem sighed, feeling and now understanding her frustration and shame.

"I'm sorry," Jarem said. "That is a lot to take in."

But on the inside, Jarem still felt hope. Whatever happened was not Zelwa's doing or her fault. He could feel no ill intent from her. She had to be an innocent bystander. But, the fact she could disarm the resurrects...well, that was amazing.

"I don't want to rush you," Jarem said. "There may be more resurrects inside the cave, but there are definitely some outside. I can't forget my friends are out there. I have to help them. I don't know that there is much I can do, but...*you* could. If you are willing to."

"When I get close to them, I can feel them. Do you think they can feel me, too?"

"I don't know the answers. But you seem to be the only thing that can stop them."

Jarem felt some relief. He had been worried that the burden was all on him to figure this out and then fight the resurrects. It was nice to have that pressure off. It gave him the strength to be more courageous.

"I've been waiting for this moment for so long. I thought it would be me having to charge out there. Alone. Probably to die, but to hopefully achieve something. And now there is you. We can do this together if you're willing. I can't decide for you and I won't force you. But I hope we can take back the right of our species to live and thrive without fear. And you should be able to take back what was stolen from you. We can't get your family back, but you can take back your power."

Zelwa stood and leaned against the cave wall. She looked like she was thinking of something. Jarem tried to get a feel for it. It was as if there was something she wanted to protect.

Zelwa was quiet for several moments. Jarem felt time ticking away slowly. Finally, she nodded.

"I can't let them continue. And I need to feel whole again. I'm still alive. I have to do something."

Jarem felt himself connect with her a little. It was enough for him to trust her.

"Let's take the fight straight to them," Zelwa said. "We'll go out the main entrance to the cave. They are waiting there. I'm sure of it."

Jarem nodded. His stomach knotted up, but he took strength in the knowledge of what Zelwa could do, what she had already done.

He took her hand, and they both moved with new determination to face the resurrects head on.

CHAPTER 16: THINGS ARE GETTING REAL
ZELWA

"I think you should get behind me," Zelwa said as they approached the cave exit.

Jarem moved behind her and she steeled herself for what would come next. Zelwa opened the door and was surprised when there were no resurrects there. Jarem moved around her quickly, alarmed. The small spacecraft was there, but apparently empty.

"My friends!" he shouted and began running down the path that led to the ship and then the stone arch.

Zelwa joined him. She couldn't help but think of the last time she was running down this path with Mora.

Zelwa ran into Jarem as they rounded the hill where the ship was hidden. He had stopped suddenly, and it didn't take long for her to see why. The ship was closed, but there were two teens, a girl and boy standing outside of it. They turned to look up at Zelwa and Jarem.

Zelwa felt her energy coming from them, but something was different. Their eyes were not blood red, just a hint of red glow, and their bodies had not been damaged.

Jarem's body went rigid in front of Zelwa as the two teens rose off the ground and floated up within ten feet of them and then settled back on the ground.

The girl and boy looked Zelwa up and down. Their movements appeared to be synchronized, but only the girl spoke.

"I have been looking for you," she said. "I felt you in the forming and then in the big space. You have eluded me all this time. But," the girl and boy stretched their arms over their heads as if they had just awakened, "I don't know that I need you now. I don't know why I thought I ever needed you. These two are still in here," both girl and boy put their hand to the center of their upper chest, "but their attachment allows me to use these bodies and contain myself. I've never had access to this feeling before."

"They are still in there?" Jarem asked.

The boy and girl nodded.

"It is useful, but they require more efforts." The teens made a face. "The living tissue requires nutrients. I don't know how long they will last. I must find more to continue this experience."

Zelwa felt Jarem's hand on her arm, gripping it tightly. Zelwa was a little freaked out that the resurrects had been looking for her.

"Who are you?" Zelwa asked. In a smaller voice she said, "You're not Mora?"

"What is Mora?"

"She would have been the first body you...," Zelwa wasn't sure how to finish. She thought of Mora, her friend. The last she saw of Mora, she was in a trance. Maybe she wasn't scared. Maybe she didn't know or feel anything.

"The first vessel," the girl said with what appeared to be a fond smile. It was eerie how both the girl and boy moved in sync, even when only the girl spoke. "Is the word Mother? Yes, she gave birth to us."

"I don't know what she did or why, but she wouldn't have wanted you to kill everyone," Zelwa spat.

"Kill?" the girl said. "We only survived. And grew as a child grows. A mother would want her child to grow. Their bodies are still in existence, the ones we entered. They are kept in stasis by my energy."

My energy, Zelwa thought. Zelwa imagined Mora's body still floating in space. Mora wouldn't have wanted that, either. Zelwa considered what she should do next. She could feel her energy in these two more strongly than it had been in the resurrects, but it also didn't feel as eager to flow from them back to her.

"Mora. Mother," the girl was saying as if remembering. "Perhaps I shall take her name for myself. A memorial for her sacrifice and gift."

"Her name is Kin! And his is Tock!" Jarem spat out, coming to life. "They have their own lives."

The Kin and Tock creatures turned their attention to Jarem.

"Kin. Tock. Yes. Worthy vessels. They are Mora now."

"Where are the others?"

"Others?" Kin-Mora asked. "The ones like you," she looked at Jarem, "the ones I can inhabit?" The Moras both looked to the ship. "They are being fetched for me. When they are found and entered, this ship will be ours. We will need it for the many I will become."

"We won't let that happen," Jarem said with determination.

"This planet is holding something back from me," Kin-Mora said, ignoring Jarem and looking down at the ground. They glanced at Zelwa. "What is under the surface?" The Moras knelt and placed a hand on the ground. Zelwa noticed the nearby rocks trembling. The Moras looked at Zelwa again. "*Who* is under there?"

Before Zelwa could respond, she noticed the rocky surface the Mora was touching was opening up in a hole. Zelwa realized she would have to act fast before those things found the protected Earthers below the surface.

"You have something of mine," Zelwa said. "And I want it back."

196

The Mora paused in making the hole and stood.

At least it stopped them for now, Zelwa thought.

"This new perspective is interesting. I could not communicate before. I didn't really understand what that would be like until I found these two bodies. You are not very supportive in your current state. You will be. I will have this one," the creatures looked at Jarem, then turned to Zelwa. "And I will have you as well. I can have everything." She looked down. "Even what this planet holds."

Zelwa steeled herself to pull at her energy. She felt a trickle moving back to her. A shiver passed through the Moras and they smiled. Then only the girl was smiling.

"Ah, the next evolution," Kin-Mora said. Tock-Mora ceased his parroting and knelt to open the hole further. The girl remained standing and faced Jarem and Zelwa.

With no actual plan or other options, Zelwa began pulling harder at her energy. The energy felt tied to an anchor. She pulled and pulled at it, but it didn't flow back to her like it had with the other resurrects.

"Communicating is over, then," Kin-Mora said. "Too bad. I enjoy the stimulation. But, I will adjust."

Zelwa felt an energetic yank that almost pulled her physical body forward and then her energy began slipping out and away from her.

CHAPTER 17: RAISING THE STAKES
JAREM

The voice of the Kin-Mora was unnerving to Jarem. It looked like Kin and was using her voice, but it had a strange extra vibration to it. It chilled Jarem to the bone. They were talking to the thing, the being, that had killed so many Earthers.

He tried to focus on the details of the situation. It hadn't tried to take him and Zelwa right away. He sensed it was enjoying the interaction. Also, it had said that Kin and Tock were still inside. With the bodies not damaged, maybe there was a chance of getting them back.

The resurrect seemed more vulnerable in this form. When red-eyed and hovering over the ground, they were as terrifying to look at as to know what they could do. It also occurred to him why there was a spaceship. The Kin and Tock resurrect forms weren't protected by the same field as the torn bodies. They weren't completely consumed by whatever this thing was. He didn't want to hurt Kin or Tock, but knowing that the resurrect wasn't completely protected in this form could be useful.

As the resurrect, the Mora, was talking, Jarem reached out to it telepathically. Using the mind and body of the Earther was new to it, and maybe he could use that to his advantage. He probed, looking for something in the Mora's consciousness to use against it. Initially, he felt an overwhelming confidence that had developed after hundreds of years of nothing standing in its way. He kept probing, knowing that they were so close and that there had to be something.

He felt something familiar within the Mora. Maybe a remnant of Kin and Tock floating in the energy. He floated with them. It felt as if they were leading him to something. And finally, he felt something different. Something useful. Even through all of its confidence, the Mora had a fear. It feared ceasing to exist. That fear had driven it all those years to travel through space, to expand and protect what it had expanded into. It was looking to connect to the source of its energy–Zelwa–but it hadn't been able to locate her and so tapped into all that was like her.

Now that Jarem had the ammo he needed, he went to work. As the Kin-Mora focused on Zelwa, he sent an idea, the idea of reincarnation. Perhaps it would be distracted by the idea of an opportunity to return in another form.

When it looked like Zelwa began pulling at her power, Jarem increased his attack, adding in doubt whether their actions would lead to a more negative life in the next incarnation. He thought he was making some headway when Zelwa gasped. Jarem could see that she was growing weaker. He could feel her presence drifting away as if she wasn't there.

Jarem directed his focus back at the Kin-Mora. He glanced over at Tock-Mora. The hole it was forming had gone deep underground and had opened into a cave. Jarem thought he heard footsteps running and yelling.

He turned to look at Kin-Mora again and it was looking at him and smiling the same pleased smile he had seen at the portal.

"Kin?"

"Tock?"

The two names came from two different voices. Jarem watched as Rema and Nelly slipped out from behind some boulders. They must have trapped the other resurrects inside the ship and gotten away.

Kin-Mora looked at the ship in confusion.

"Yeah, we're not in there," Nelly said. "And we're not going to let you take any more of us." Nelly charged forward.

"Nelly, wait," Rema said. "We have to work together--"

It was too late. Nelly was running at Kin-Mora. Just as she got within arm's length, she stopped abruptly and collapsed. She looked over at Jarem, her face strained. She was fighting, but it didn't look like she was winning. Jarem tried to increase his efforts. Peripherally, he could see Rema focused and adding to his telepathic attack. Nelly turned her head enough to see Tock-Mora, the hole nearly the width of an

Earther's height. Jarem saw her tears before her body convulsed and stilled.

"Nooooo!" Jarem screamed.

Nelly's body twitched, and she rose, the now familiar red glow in her eyes. Nelly-Mora stood near Kin-Mora. Nelly-Mora reached out and touched Kin-Mora's face. They smiled and nodded at one another. Nelly-Mora turned to Rema, who was straining at her effort.

Jarem felt the same strain as Kin-Mora focused on him again. This time, he felt the attack. Some foreign energy was forcing itself in—not just his mind, but throughout his body. He remembered how it felt at the portal, when the tendril of what he suspected was the resurrect began forcing its way in.

His energy shifted to defense in the same way he had worked with Dr. Yac. Jarem went straight to the memory that held the most power for him, the one that anchored him. He played the memory over and over in mind in excruciating detail.

He could see his mother's face in his mind as if she was still there in front of him, kissing his forehead.

"No sounds, remember?" she had said. "I love you. And it will be okay."

She had closed off the opening in the wall. Jarem felt anger at the loss. And some anger at his mother for leaving him, even knowing she had made the only choice in a bad situation. She didn't really know that he would be okay. And he certainly hadn't felt okay when Sloctum snatched him up and brought him to Hanu to go on the selling block.

He had more love for her than anger. She had given up her life and protected him. She didn't know he would be okay, but the idea had stayed with him and he had had faith in her declaration. And he was okay. Even with his fear and doubt. He had friends. He had a mission. Her face was in his mind again and he felt a warmth and light surrounding it.

"I love you. It will be okay."

The words were as clear in his mind as the day she had said them. He felt her love flowing over him and through him like a protective barrier.

And...he realized amid his emotions...Kin-Mora had not taken him over yet. For the moment, he was still Jarem, and, for now, he still had control over his mind and body.

CHAPTER 18: ENOUGH IS ENOUGH

ZELWA

As the Kin-Mora pulled at Zelwa's energy, Zelwa felt part of herself shift out of her body and float upwards. She looked down, seeing her physical body hunching over, then dropping to its knees. She realized she could no longer feel her arms and legs, and she wondered for a moment if she had ever left the arch. Could all of this have been a scene like she experienced with her mom and dad?

This felt different. She couldn't feel her arms and legs, but she could see a translucent version of them as she floated up further and observed the scene from above.

The experience was like pushing against soft waves in the ocean with the tide still trying to pull you out. The Kin-Mora was still in front of her and the Nelly-Mora had Rema on her knees. Jarem was also on his knees. The Tock-Mora seemed a little stressed—his face pinched tight. Zelwa saw the hole was getting smaller instead of bigger. *The people underground must be trying to stop them from getting in!*

Zelwa watched as Rema collapsed and then rose as part of the Mora. She joined Nelly and Kin-Mora, and they all faced Jarem. Zelwa tried to think of something she could do to help. She floated over the Mora, but they didn't even register her presence and she couldn't contact them. Annoyed, she floated higher again. Something flickered above the Mora and caught her eye, then it was gone. She floated around trying to see it again and finally caught it—a thin thread of energy trailing from the Mora and floating away. Zelwa noted that a similar thread was floating away from her body. Both strands were floating in the same direction. Zelwa followed it and found herself at the arch. Dr. Yac was there with Peet and Stavo.

"I can't leave them," Peet was telling Dr. Yac. Stavo appeared deep in thought. He sat on a boulder near the arch, watching Dr. Yac and Peet.

"You promised your friends you would be the one to go," Dr. Yac was saying. "You must honor that. You will be needed to pass on the training to the other Earthers on Hanu."

Zelwa stopped listening as she saw where the threads ended together, twisted and entangled in the arch's opening. She had the thought that if she untangled them, the Mora would lose most of its power since it was leeching it from her. The only way she could see to do it would be to destroy the arch. Unfortunately, she didn't have a body or a way to tell anyone.

She tried connecting in a telepathic way with Peet but he didn't seem to notice.

"You have a strange energy around you," Dr. Yac said, but Zelwa couldn't get any information to him either. It really sucked not having a voice or body to communicate with!

Maybe Jarem will be more receptive, she thought.

Zelwa remembered how things had shifted when she was in the dream world. She thought of Jarem, focused on his location, and found herself there with him. She tried to tell him that the arch needed to be destroyed. She sent images of it to him. She was at a loss at what else to try. Jarem was waning, and it didn't appear that she was getting through to him either. That he was holding out at all was actually astounding after all that he had told her about the resurrects.

Zelwa noticed her body crumpling on the ground. She wondered what would happen when they could finally pull out every bit. Would her body die? Would she become one of them? The energy wasn't pushing her out and filling her up like it did with the others. She thought the energy might eventually unplug from her body. Would she just die? And would that be so bad? What was she fighting so hard for? Everyone she knew was dead. Maybe it would be easier to join them.

No, Zelwa thought. *They took my life from me. I won't let them take any more!*

Zelwa thought herself back to the arch, unsure what she could do but knowing the next action needed to happen there. She had to destroy the arch. She floated over it, looking down, the energy in the threads pulsing against one another. *Maybe they couldn't survive without her. Maybe she should allow herself to die so it would be over.*

That thought held sway for a minute, but she wanted to live. Didn't what she wanted matter?

"The arch," Dr. Yak says. "Jarem says to break the arch."

Did I get through? Zelwa thought. *I must have gotten through to him.* Excited, she hovered over the arch, waiting.

"How...?"

Peet ran over to the arch and tried to push it over. He switched on a laser from his wristband to cut the stone, but the laser never touched it-it bounced off unharmed.

"Something's stopping me from-" Peet said.

Zelwa's frustration grew again as nothing Peet did had any effect on the arch.

"We can help," a voice said.

Zelwa watched as Thames and three other people from the underground walked into the area.

"Where did you come from?"

Dr. Yac's skin turned a deep purple in surprise.

"Explanations later," Thames said. "Let us do our part." He nodded to the three people with him and they surrounded the arch, then knelt and touched the ground around it. The stone of the arch trembled.

"I can't live like this anymore," Stavo said to no one in particular and ran.

Zelwa wondered where he would go, but was distracted as the arch crumbled and fell. She felt herself growing heavy and being pulled back into her body. The ground felt cool as she opened her eyes and pushed herself up. She tugged at her energy with all her might. This time, it flowed back to her like a waterfall following the pull of gravity.

Jarem released a ragged breath and Zelwa saw him stand as he braced himself to face his friends.

Then, just as suddenly as it flowed, Zelwa's energy slowed again. The Mora weren't done fighting. She saw Jarem's body tense. Zelwa pulled and pulled, hoping to give him some relief. She wasn't sure what else they could do when Stavo walked up. He passed between Jarem and Zelwa and walked right up to the Mora.

Zelwa thought the Mora were as surprised as she and Jarem were when Stavo punched the Kin-Mora in the face. The Kin-Mora fell, stunned, unaccustomed to physical contact and harm from other beings.

"That is for my mother." Stavo turned to Zelwa and Jarem. "And for all of you."

Zelwa watched Jarem dart forward and before the Mora could come to its senses and attack again, he placed his hand on the Kin-Mora's head.

Zelwa followed his lead and began drawing in her energy with all her might. She felt it coming in trickles and streams from not just the Mora in front of her, but from every direction. She caught glimpses in her mind of resurrect bodies collapsing where they floated, the energy that had been protecting their cells and body parts flowing out of them and back to her. As the energy left them, the bodies fell apart into dust, into molecules, into seeming nothingness. The resurrect presence was disappearing throughout the cosmos.

CHAPTER 19: IS THIS THE REAL LIFE?
JAREM

Jarem sifted around in the Kin-Mora's mind for Kin.
The other Mora tried to attack him and Stavo. Even the
Tock-Mora gave up on the hole that was closing faster
than he could open it. Stavo was keeping them off
balance with little effort. They did not know how to
use a physical body to attack or protect, but in
attacking them physically, they weren't able to focus
on a telepathic attack. Jarem could easily fend them
off when they got close to him, all the while keeping
his hand on Kin-Mora while he searched for remnants
of his friend.

He worked on distracting it again with thoughts of an afterlife and reincarnating into something greater. It wasn't fighting him as hard as before. And he could see Zelwa growing more confident as she pulled in her energy. He felt the glow of her presence even from the distance he was from her.

It wasn't long before Jarem felt the boundaries of what was the Mora in Kin's mind. It was contracting and getting smaller as he probed. Then it convulsed into something bigger. Jarem watched as Rema collapse. It convulsed again, and Nelly fell. Then Tock. Their bodies lay still on the ground and Jarem felt a pang in his chest.

Zelwa breathed a sigh of relief.

"I feel like I have all that is me back."

"There is still something here and I can't leave it here in Kin," Jarem said. He was also watching the bodies of his friends for movement. At the moment, there was none. He wondered if he would have to sacrifice Kin as well to get rid of the Mora's energy. He wasn't sure he could do that.

Zelwa walked over and placed her hand on Kin-Mora's heart.

"The energy that formed the resurrects started in the stone of this planet," she said. "Maybe we can transfer it out and back into the stone."

"Can you do that?" Jarem asked.

"I don't know that I can," Zelwa said. She backed away from Kin-Mora. "I might cause something bad to happen. Something worse."

"Just because bad things happen, it does not mean that you cause it," a now familiar voice said. "Maybe it doesn't even mean it is bad."

Zelwa turned to see Thames walking up to her.

"After Mora did what she did," Thames went on, "our ancestors had an exponential jump in their understanding. The next generation understood more and were more open. We grew the caves to our needs. We are the rock-molders. The adapters."

"Can you help his friend?" Zelwa asked.

"We can do it together," Thames said. "Then this cycle can close."

Zelwa was silent. Thames picked up a nearby stone the size of a fist. He placed it in Zelwa's hands and put one of his hands over it. Jarem watched with curiosity.

"Can you continue to hold the energy as you are doing?" Thames asked Jarem.

"If it saves my friend, I will hold it as long as necessary," Jarem said. He could feel the resurrect energy trying to find a chink in the boundary, but it was much weaker now and Jarem held it easily.

"Good, brother," Thames said. He placed his other hand around Zelwa's, so that they both cupped the rock in their hands. "Now, sister," he said, softly. "Let's Impress it back from whence it came."

Zelwa nodded. Jarem noticed tears were streaming down her cheeks. He hazarded a check on her and felt something akin to openness and gratitude. Jarem felt grateful, too, but it seemed different for Zelwa. Deeper.

"We start with the breathing," Thames said.

Zelwa laughed through her tears. She breathed deeply.

"I know, but thank you for the reminder," she said. "Let's press forward into the next thing." She smiled at Thames. He nodded and they closed their eyes.

Jarem watched as Zelwa and Thames began breathing in sync with one another and drifted into a meditative state. Several long moments passed. He could still feel the resurrect energy inside of Kin. He waited and waited. The stone in their hands emitted a soft light that turned red and then purple and back to white. As the color was shifting, Jarem felt a release inside Kin, and the resurrect energy poured out of her as if from one cup to another.

Thames and Zelwa opened up their hands to look at the stone. With a long bang, it cracked open in Zelwa's hand. She jumped and dropped it. As it hit the ground, green matter spread out of the rock and along the ground. It started as a moss and became grass, and it spread over everything they could see.

"What's happening?" Zelwa asked.

Jarem was startled as well. It was an odd sensation to feel the softness of vegetation forming under his feet and see it around the bodies of his friends. And then he felt it in each of them. The soul-part that was them was flowing back through their bodies. They were moving and awakening.

Jarem watched as a pool of water formed nearby. Small shrubs sprouted out of the ground and he could see small trees forming in the distance. It was as if the planet was coming to life. It didn't seem possible, yet he was watching it happen.

Jarem watched Thames walk over to stare at the pool of water.

"Do you understand what is happening?" Jarem asked Thames. Jarem was surprised at the presence of another Earther, but he didn't seem to be a threat.

Thames nodded in the negative.

"I've never seen so much water gathered together like this," he said. "It makes me strangely uncomfortable."

"It can be fun," Zelwa said, elbowing Thames as if he were an old friend. Maybe he was? Jarem didn't know. "But learn to swim first. And make sure someone is around to watch you. I can help you with both those things if you'd like."

Jarem didn't understand the exchange, but he had more pressing matters. His friends were pushing themselves up into a seated position. He and Stavo had to hit them several times, and they were feeling their sore muscles as they regained control of their bodies.

"Was I in a fight?" Tock asked, rubbing his abdomen and jaw. He looked around at Jarem in surprise. "Did you come back?" Without waiting for an answer, he stood and looked over the planet. "This isn't Hanu."

Tock was then nearly knocked off his feet again by Nelly, who pummeled him with a forceful hug. Rema had moved over to Kin and was holding her. Kin seemed the most affected and weak. Of course, the resurrects had controlled her the longest.

Peet joined the group, checking in with Rema first. Dr. Yac followed and stood by Jarem.

"We did it," Jarem said. Dr. Yac bowed his head in acknowledgement. "We did it!" Jarem shouted to his team. They all turned to him. "We did it," Jarem said, much softer. He took in everyone—his team, Zelwa, Thames, and even Stavo. "We all did it."

"Indeed, it is done." They all turned to see the enormous figure of Elder standing amongst them. "This planet is in the next phase of its evolution." Elder looked them all over. "And so are you all."

Thames nodded as if Elder had said the most logical thing. Something didn't seem right to Jarem. He thought of what Zelwa had said about Elder cultivating the planet.

"Did you cause this?" Jarem asked.

Even Dr. Yac's eyes widened at the possibility. He stared at Elder.

"I did nothing but allow things to unfold as they did," Elder responded.

Dr. Yac stepped forward. "You allowed this planet to be seeded through the decimation of a species?"

"The essence of what you said is true. I *allowed* it. I did not cause it."

"You brought them here. You were waiting for something like this to happen."

"They wanted to be here. I never know quite how things will evolve. Each planet attracts exactly what it needs to shift into the next stage."

"Each planet?" Dr. Yac said. "Who are you to play such games with an entire species?"

Jarem watched as Dr. Yac and Elder stared at one another.

This was the most Jarem had ever seen a Yacca speak on their behalf. He was sure more dialogue was happening telepathically, but he couldn't make out anything. Jarem tried to probe, but was cut off from their thoughts. He also realized that he was unbelievably tired from everything they had been through.

After several moments, Dr. Yac stepped back, standing in awe of Elder.

"I understand," is all Dr. Yac would say.

CHAPTER 20: AND NOW?
ZELWA

"It's odd," Jarem was saying to Zelwa. "Dr. Yak says that all life growing here appears to be vegetative. The vegetation doesn't appear to require insects or anything else to flourish. And none seems to be harmful to Earthers."

They were walking along what was now a green pathway on the planet's surface. Many of the people from inside the caves were exploring the surface as well, though they still felt the caves were their homes.

"Elder says the planet has been encoded with our DNA," Zelwa explained, running her hand along a

221

mossy rock. It felt cool and alive and such a difference to how dusty it had been before. "And, it seems, according to how we are evolved now, we don't need the same challenges that we faced on Earth."

Jarem nodded. *He doesn't seem fazed by anything*, Zelwa thought. She could only imagine what he and his friends had lived through—what all Earthers had survived. And not survived. Zelwa noticed Jarem was looking at her again. She'd caught him doing that more and more. It was an odd sensation.

"What?" she said.

"I don't know if we've talked about it," Jarem said. "But one of my 'evolutions' is that I can read what others are feeling. And sometimes what they are thinking."

Zelwa suddenly felt embarrassed. Had she thought anything weird? It was a lot to know that Elder and other higher beings could read your mind. She wasn't sure how she felt about another human doing so.

"I didn't mean to make you embarrassed," Jarem said with a smile. "I won't pry into your thoughts or emotions. I just wanted you to know. And if you ever wanted to see if you can do the same, I'd be happy to help you."

Zelwa frowned. She wasn't sure that would be something she would want to do. She also wondered if that ability would have helped things along with her parents. She often thought of what she had seen in their memories and how she had encountered them in the dreaming state she had been in. Zelwa looked at Jarem. He was still smiling, not in a creepy way, it was more reassuring than anything. She didn't feel he would force her to do anything she didn't want to. After all they had been through, she felt safe trusting him.

"I'll think about it," she said. "But does that mean you plan to stay here for a while?" It surprised her to notice that she hoped he would. It had only been two days on Laris since what was being called The Greening. They found a spot in the grass to sit and watch the wind blowing through the small trees that had grown unnaturally fast.

"It has been nice to not run and to know we won't have the resurrects to contend with," Jarem said. "But we still have work to do. The rest of the galaxy doesn't know yet. We have other Earthers to free. Maybe some of them would want to come here. Maybe they would want to go back to visit or recolonize Earth." He looked at Zelwa. "Maybe you would want to come with us."

Zelwa felt something connect in their minds and she saw the image of a familiar blue planet in her imagination. She smiled. If she went back, she would know things that no one else knew. They could speculate, but she had actually lived there. Her parents had instilled in her a love of history and developing civilization. What could she save and pass on?

"I think your parents would be proud," Jarem said.

"Did you just...?"

"Sorry," Jarem said. "I didn't intend to, but the image and feelings were so strong."

Zelwa thought about it for a few moments.

"Earth has probably changed so much," she finally said.

"Then we can explore it," Jarem said. "I feel exploration maybe in your genetics."

Zelwa smiled. She thought about her mom and dad and their travels. Travel could be risky. She thought about Thames and all the people inside Laris. She felt like something had healed within her when she and Thames had come together to perform the Impressing—like she had finally become reconciled to her family. It was odd that it had happened so quickly. In that moment, everything that had gone before seemed insignificant, and the only way forward was to let go of her guilt and shame and focus on what needed to be done so that the future would be better.

Zelwa took a deep breath, one fragrant with newly grown flowers. For now, Laris seemed like a safe place to stay. Why would she risk herself in the unknown? She looked up into the sky, which was blue now instead of the dusty orange it had been before. Were they still taking their species forward? What happened if you stay dormant?

"Is that what you want to do?" Zelwa asked Jarem.

"Maybe," Jarem said. "That's the most amazing part. We get to decide." He lay back on the grass, looking up into the sky.

"We get to decide," Zelwa said. She lay back on the grass, too, still feeling safe and content for the moment. She looked over at Jarem and smiled. He smiled back. Zelwa could feel a tiny tremor along the ground as if the planet was still stretching in its evolution. Her back grew warm with the new life forming all around them.

ABOUT THE AUTHOR

Sheila Lee Brown is a writer, artist, and generally very curious person. She spent her childhood playing outdoors in the woods surrounding her home and making up stories with her three siblings.

Sheila currently lives with her husband and their dog and enjoys writing, reading, drawing silly cartoons, and always learning and growing.

You can find out more about her upcoming projects at: www.sheilaleebrown.com

NOTE FROM THE AUTHOR

Thank you for reading my book! I don't think of myself as a sci-fi writer, but this idea got a hold of me. It stemmed from a dream where I was on a spaceship and surrounded by the type of resurrect creature described in this story. I was unnerved, but then realized I could pull energy from them. They collapsed and I prevailed. The scenario intrigued me enough to want to create something from it.

When I first starting writing this, it was just going to be one book, but now I know there will be more. Stay tuned!

If you enjoyed reading this book, would you please take a moment to leave me a review at your favorite retailer?

Thanks, and best wishes!
-Sheila

www.ingramcontent.com/pod-product-compliance
Lightning Source LLC
Chambersburg PA
CBHW051433170626
46809CB00006B/2441